*A Portrait
of Myself*

A Portrait of Myself

A NOVEL BY
WINIFRED MADISON

Random House · New York

Library of Congress Cataloging in Publication Data
Madison, Winifred.   A Portrait of Myself.
SUMMARY: Though possessing artistic ability, sixteen-year-old Catherine, suffering from a broken home, socialization problems, and a teacher's disfavor, finally attempts suicide. [1. Artists—Fiction. 2. Teachers—Fiction. 3. Suicide—Fiction] I. Title.   PZ7.M2652Po   [Fic]   78-13897
ISBN: 0-394-84021-6 (trade)   ISBN: 0-394-94021-0 (lib. bdg.)
Manufactured in the United States of America.   1 2 3 4 5 6 7 8 9 0

For Mariucca

A Portrait
of Myself

Prologue

A full-length portrait of myself, Catherine d'Amato, painted when I was six, has always hung on the wall of my bedroom. The cheap newsprint from which it was cut now curls between the tacks and the colors are fading, but the solemn dark eyes, embellished with carefully drawn eyelashes, still gaze out at the world. The tiny gold earrings remain pinned in each earlobe under a hive of scrawled black ringlets.

"Why do you hang on to that old thing? It was cute once, but it's a mess now. Besides, you're fifteen, not six," my mother complained again and again last year.

I always shrugged my shoulders. There was no point in explaining to her that for me this early portrait was a relic. She would answer, "A *relic*? What do you mean, a relic? You think you're a saint or something?"

She could not understand her only daughter, a difficult child.

Nor did she remember how she hugged me and called me her cute little darling, her sweet *cara cara,* when I showed her the portrait and how she could not wait to boast about it

to my father when he came home from work. The two of
them stood in the small kitchen on Ravenna Street and
beamed at me.

Yes, the portrait was just that, a relic of a happier time, a
more innocent place, an Eden in which I lived. On that warm
day in May when Miss Bowen, my first-grade teacher, traced
our outlines on newsprint and we filled in the essential features of our first self-portraits, I overheard her remark to
another teacher.

"This one, the d'Amato child, has a gift."

A gift? What kind of gift I could not imagine, since it was
neither Christmas nor my birthday. I suspected it had something to do with my drawing. The two teachers smiled at
me in a kindly way, singling me out, and I carried the assur-
ance of this mysterious gift within me like a happy secret.

Imagine thirty first-graders dragging their likenesses behind them through River Street and Commercial Street on
their way home after school. Even the old crones who
perched in upstairs windows all day to watch who came and
who went in the street below allowed themselves to smile
down at us. Two old men sitting on kitchen chairs placed on
the sidewalk so they could sun themselves made me stop to
show them my portrait, then praised me in a melodious flow
of Italian.

River Street, Front Street, Ravenna Street, Commercial
Street...a small Italian village transported to a city in
Connecticut. Now it seems to me that it was a paradise.
Never was a place more alive with people walking up and
down the streets all day and most of the night. Nowhere else
were there such smells, such sounds, such colors. Long loaves
of freshly baked bread were placed in the windows of the
Stella Bakery each day, and the delicious fragrance wafted
into the crowded streets. Somewhere else, the smell of wine.

On the corner a fruit-and-vegetable stand gone mad with color. And always music, always the sound of Italian, always a traffic jam with the honking of horns and the ceaseless flow of conversation of women shopping, women standing at the street corner and admiring each other's babies.

I had hundreds of relations—more aunts, uncles, and cousins than I could count, and those "almost-relatives" who came from the same village in Italy as my grandparents. In our family I seemed almost to be an only child, for my brother, Vincent, had little patience with a younger sister. But I made up for this lack of attention by seeking out my cousins, who were always in plentiful supply. Among them was Gloria, the most adored of Aunt Carol's three daughters, the one who always wore the prettiest dresses and who won every child beauty contest that came along. Anthony, more of a brother to me than my real brother, played the violin "like an angel," so I was told, a remark I took literally, seeing in my mind's eye violin-playing angels with wide green eyes and long noses, like Anthony's. But mostly I played with Joanna, my quick sloe-eyed cousin, and this did not please my mother in the least. She could not forbid me to play with a relative, but she warned me more than once, "She's not a good one. You be careful of her. Don't see her so much. With all the cousins you have, why you must pick Joanna. . . ." And so on.

But I didn't listen. It was Joanna I liked, Joanna with whom I dawdled along Front Street, mingling with the crowds there. How petted we were, how spoiled!

" 'allo, Caterina. *Come stai,* Giovanna?" The grocer gave me colored chalk so I could draw pictures on the sidewalk, not in front of his store, please, but across the street. The priest patted our heads and asked if we were good girls; I was never completely sure but Joanna always nodded her head virtuously, though she might have just stolen a plum from the grocer. Fat Maria, who worked in the bakery, could always be wheedled out of a fluted pink and green cookie. Even the "bird lady," a skinny, harmlessly deranged young woman who tripped along the street, arms outspread as she whistled bird calls, broke out of her revery long enough to smile at us.

Not everyone loved us, however. I was afraid of the boys who followed us and made fun of us. One in particular, Tommy Bacco, taunted me, calling me "Monkey, monkey!" And it was Joanna who taught me not to burst into tears but to run up to him and kick him in the shins.

I could sigh for the sweetness of what I remember of how it was in the old neighborhood. My mother sang while she scrubbed the small, dark apartment on Ravenna Street; she filled the windows with plants that she coaxed sweetly until they blossomed as if enchanted. Each week my father took me walking along River Street, where the produce market bloomed like a garden. Once he bought me a peach, choosing the biggest one he could find, and afterward he wiped my chin as the juice dripped down.

But as I grew older my memories became less sweet. My parents fought more and more, she screaming, and he answering in low, sullen tones that frightened me more than her loud complaints. More than once, with my hands over my ears, I ran to the shoe-repair shop on the next block where my uncle John and aunt Flora welcomed me, for they knew about my parents' fights and probably felt sorry for me.

"Hello, Catherine! How nice! You wanna see Tony? Go upstairs. He's practicing. You can listen to him." This they obviously considered a privilege.

I climbed the stairs to their apartment and sat perfectly still beside the rubber tree in the parlor while Anthony played his violin, winking at me between scales and dizzying flights of notes. Later, when I thought my parents had probably stopped fighting, I whispered good-bye to Tony, slipped downstairs, and went home.

Home was home. I did not think in terms of loving it or hating it; it was there. I fled from it when fighting began and when my father scolded my brother. But I loved it too, especially when my aunt Carol and my aunt Mary came to sit with my mother in the kitchen or when they gathered to make ravioli, while I played with my cousins. At such times everything was all right. It was possible to be content.

Nothing lasts forever. The city decided to renew the section where we lived. Freeways had to be built; the tired old buildings had to be torn down to make room for high glass industrial towers; and the narrow streets were to be broken up, widened, and changed beyond recognition. Drawings of the new city that would replace our village appeared in the newspapers.

Where would we go? Wherever we could find a place to live. One by one the buildings were vacated, then torn down. People who had been neighbors for years embraced with tears and then parted from one another. Ravenna Street was dug up, totally destroyed, as if it had never existed. Joanna and I stood together when the bulldozer flattened our apartment house to a heap of rubble. It took less than an hour. Later the land on which the building stood was made into a six-story parking lot.

Many of the Italians moved to the south end of the city, but my father insisted on moving us to a mixed neighborhood, Lily Street, where no lilies grew. He found an apartment for us in an older three-story brick house on a cheerless street that led to a prisonlike factory. It gave us a place to live, but it was never home. After two years, when I was twelve, my father left home and a year later so did my brother.

At sixteen, my mother and I still lived together in the same apartment on Lily Street. For me it was a time of confusion and restlessness I did not understand.

Chapter One

My sixteenth summer was the time when I longed to fall in love but there was nobody to fall in love with. I dreamed of a boy with a shock of blond hair and incredibly deep blue eyes, someone named Eric or Sven, someone I'd never met before.

The mirror played games with me, particularly the many mirrors at the Mona Lisa Salon of Beauty, where I worked. They reflected a tall, slender girl with a cascade of pale, smooth hair that spread over her shoulders and fell down her back. Clear blue eyes sometimes green and sometimes violet. A transparent skin delicately tanned to the shade of clear honey. Serene as a tall pine by a mountain stream, slick as an advertisement.

Mirages don't last. The next minute the real Catherine appeared in the mirror, more like twelve than sixteen, with eyes that were too large and dark, and a crow's nest of black hair. If only I were beautiful like my cousin Gloria! If only I were smart like my friend Rita Blomberg! If only I had real drawing talent like Ed Magill! I made a face at the real Catherine, a monkey grimace.

"But you're so cute! And you have such marvelous eyes!"

Mrs. Russo, who owns the Mona Lisa, had told me that more than once. She longed to "make me over." "If only you weren't so serious, Catherine! Young girls should be light, happy, laughing!"

It was exactly what my mother said and Aunt Carol echoed. They would drive me out of my mind. When they weren't around, I experimented.

Flirting with my image, I turned my head away slightly, lifted an eyebrow, and coaxed a smile. There, was I light? Happy? Impossible. A monkey with a small nose that seems to ask a question as it turns up, that's what I am. The chin, too small but firm, even stubborn. And then there was that bushel of hair! I didn't know what to do with it.

"Don't complain so much," my mother said. It was easy for her to say. She has a rich wavy auburn-brown softness of hair that invites caresses, while mine was a thicket. "You can only do so much with how you look, Catherine, so learn to live with it."

But I could never make peace with my image. In the end I avoided mirrors and reflections of myself in store windows and glass doors. That way I could almost believe in the tall, golden Catherine that I wished I were, a Catherine born in an open sunlit place, possibly in the country (with a stable of horses), a Catherine born of other parents, all-American parents who lived in perfect harmony and loved their straight-backed daughter, a Catherine who could stride confidently and laugh easily because, like the girls in advertisements, she was everything a girl could possibly want to be.

The day before school began, Aunt Carol, the oldest and the only rich one of the three sisters, brought over an arm-load of clothes that Gloria and her sisters had discarded. She did that every year.

"What am I going to do with that girl?" she complained

in an effort to disguise her pride in the beautiful Gloria. "She hardly wears a dress, when *pouf!* she grows out of it. She's growing so tall, Bea, you wouldn't believe it."

Of course Gloria would grow out of her clothes while I remained destined to be small forever. My mother stumbled all over herself to thank Aunt Carol, all the while explaining how expensive it was to find anything suitable for me since my "spurt of growth" had not yet begun. And so on. I sat grim-faced in a blue denim skirt and a shirt I'd worn so much it was becoming transparent. But I wasn't taking charity, not me.

"I can buy my own clothes. I do have a job," I said with a stiff lip. Aunt Carol's carefully plucked eyebrows shot up. Something new? In the past I couldn't wait to plunge into Gloria's leftovers. Now I could not stand the thought of it.

"Catherine, darling," Aunt Carol said, enunciating each syllable carefully, confidentially, "it's nothing to be ashamed of. In our family, when we were growing up, we always wore each other's clothes, didn't we, Bea? We never thought anything of it."

"Sure, I remember," my mother said in a low, gravelly voice. However, my mother had told me more than once about those clothing exchanges and how Aunt Carol was the biggest and grabbiest pig she'd ever seen. Briefly I dreamed of the golden Catherine who always chose her own clothes from the best stores. My mother, disgusted with me for not being more grateful, brought me back to the dilemma at hand.

"What's the matter with you? Any other girl would be delighted to have this opportunity." I sat in stony silence while she fingered the clothes piled on the sofa. I caught a glimpse of a plaid skirt, the sleeve of a blazer, and the frothy white of a party blouse. Everything was schoolgirl perfect with labels from Lord & Taylor and Saks Fifth Avenue. I was torn between a maddening need to try them on instantly and an irrational wish to step all over them.

"It's all right, Catherine. I understand perfectly," Aunt Carol said with unexpected sympathy. And I hated her presumption of understanding me, *perfectly* yet. "Bea, this girl is proud. It's a good character trait, not necessarily wise but not altogether bad, either. I'll leave everything here and you can do what you like. If the hems are too long, you can take them up a little."

"Thanks very much, Aunt Carol," I said, grateful for this last bit of tact. "It was very nice of you to bring this stuff over."

There, that pleased them both. My mother begged Carol to stay for a cup of espresso. "Like old times," she said.

"Sure," Aunt Carol agreed, although they both should have known that old times are really old and gone, and it's only an illusion that they can be brought back.

Then it was morning and the first day of school. I lingered before Gloria's hand-me-downs, which my mother had hung at the front of the closet where I wouldn't miss them, but resolutely I pulled out the blue denim skirt and a plain white shirt. Mine.

"Hey, Catherine," my mother called from the kitchen. "First day of school. Wear something special, huh?"

Her voice was cheerful, a good sign. I tested her moods the way sailors test the weather each morning.

"Okay, Mom." Tying a red bandanna around my neck, I walked into the kitchen. "Hey, real coffee today?"

That made it a holiday, real coffee, a grind of dark French-roast beans that filled the house with fragrance unlike the usual powdered dust we had most mornings. She also had buns warming in the oven.

"Not a red kerchief, Catherine. It makes you look too much like . . ."

"Like a monkey, is that what you mean to say?"

"Don't flare up like that," she said, flaring up herself. "You said it, not me." Reluctantly I took off the kerchief. "You know, Cath, you may not be a raving beauty, but you're cute. You could be darling. If only you'd cut your hair . . ."

Her manner, too friendly, meant a lecture was on the way, a first-day-of-school lecture. Unlike every other day, when the table was a hodgepodge of coffee cups, ashtrays, and the morning newspapers, it was now set with place mats, cups, and saucers. The scarlet rayon kimono that my mother wore opened as she leaned forward, revealing black straps straining over soft, full breasts. She had tied her hair back loosely, but a strand had escaped and curled around her neck like a tendril. I could not think she was a beautiful woman, but at that moment I saw her as Matisse might have seen her, intensely feminine and ripe. Only if he painted her there in that tiny kitchen, instead of brilliant Moroccan tapestries in the background, a clutter of groceries on uneven shelves would have to do.

Once I had asked her if she would pose for me. Immediately she had pulled together the folds of her kimono to make sure she was covered decently. "You want to paint a picture of me here, in this kitchen, wearing this stupid thing Carol gave me for Christmas eight years ago? Don't be silly. That's no way to make a picture. Wait till I get dressed. Then I'll sit in the living room. Will it take more than five minutes? Ten minutes?"

It was the kitchen mother I wanted to paint. I sat there, figuring out just how I would do it. In my mind it was becoming a warm, sensuous painting. . . .

As my mother poured the coffee, she began her annual

mother-to-daughter talk and the painting vanished. "First day of school!" she sighed. Her voice took on a warm, mellow, motherly tone. "A whole new year coming up. Lucky you! These are the best years of your life, Catherine, you better believe it."

"I don't see what's so great about them."

"Believe me. I know. The very best years. Only you don't know this until you're older. That's why I'm telling you."

"Mom, school was different when you went. You don't know what it's like now."

"Catherine, I'm not so old that I can't remember. And I don't think school is so different." She bristled, then softened again. "Okay, so it's a little worse now, crime, drugs, all that . . . it's scary . . . but nothing really changes too much. There's smart kids and stupid kids. You take care now not to be one of the stupid ones or one of the bad ones, either. Just be smart and don't waste time. You've got your whole life ahead of you, and I want you to make something of it."

"So I'm supposed to take typing and shorthand and get a job in an office, eight to five. That's making something out of my life," I said hopelessly. I'd heard the sermon before.

"It won't hurt to take accounting, too." My mother's voice rose a pitch higher, then lowered. "You got to think of the future."

"Thinking about the future makes me tired."

"Okay. But it's gonna come whether you're tired of it or not. It's there waiting and if you're not ready for it, it's your tough luck. Don't say I didn't warn you."

She shrugged her shoulders as if she had nothing to do with the laws of the universe and reached for another warm bun. She buttered it generously and evenly, like a mason spreading cement with his trowel. I wanted to put my hand over hers to stop her, because she was getting too fat; yet that would only mean another scolding. She would scream that it was none of my business; nothing would be gained. Besides, she wanted to go on with her lecture.

"Another thing, Catherine. I want you to take advantage of your opportunities."

My head sunk. I focused my eyes on her through the curly fringe on my forehead. "What opportunities?" There were none that I could see.

"Meet people. Make friends. Get out a little. And don't groan so much about typing and shorthand. School will be over before you know it. If you know enough, you can get a job in a good office, work your way up, become an executive secretary, wear good clothes, go to meetings . . ."

"Geez, Mom. That's just what I want!"

"Don't be such a sarcastic know-it-all!" The mellow motherliness of her voice was changing into an old frustration. "Do you think it's better to work in a factory and make the same thing over and over all day long?"

"You'd make more money if you worked in the factory instead of the factory office," I said and immediately regretted it. It was true that she made less money in the office, but she wore "respectable" dresses and high-heeled shoes to work and that was important to her. In a way I liked that about her, that she had her own kind of pride, even if I felt it was misplaced.

"Never mind me. Just take care of yourself," she chided me. "Now, Catherine, I want you to promise me something, one promise, that you'll take typing and shorthand."

"I suppose."

"And find new friends. You have to *try*. All you seem to know is Rita Blomberg and Joanna. I'm not so sure about Rita and thank God, Joanna is only a distant cousin, very distant, so you don't have to go with her too much. I know, you don't have to tell me, she's got plenty of hard luck, her father in prison and her mother in and out of the hospital all the time. I'm glad you're sympathetic; you got a good heart, Catherine, but don't be too chummy. That girl's gonna get into real trouble someday. As for Rita, she's nice but homely . . ."

"Mom," I interrupted. "Rita is terrific. She's gonna be somebody important someday."

"Maybe. I agree. But she's too smart, that's her trouble. Boys don't like smart girls."

"That's not really true. Maybe it was once, but times are different now."

"Ha! Different! Life keeps repeating itself, and I don't want you to repeat mine. I want you to do better. Do you understand?"

Her voice grew intense. She was practically pleading with me now. How could I "do better" when we couldn't even be compared. We were so different I couldn't understand how we came to be mother and daughter. We lived on different planets. But she was so earnest that I softened and gave her an easy promise.

"Okay, Mom. Can I have more coffee?"

"Sure. And you'll remember to sign up for typing?"

I hedged. "I'll have to ask the counselor to see if we can fit it into the schedule."

"If you want to do it, you can. One more thing, Cath. Forget about art. It was all right when you were a little kid, but you're growing up now."

No use arguing about that. I stared at my Timex pointedly.

"You're going to be late, Mom," I said, showing her my watch.

"Where's the time gone!" she cried, getting up from the table regretfully then hurrying to her bedroom. While she wriggled her way into a green print dress and stuffed her feet into black pumps that would cripple her before the day was out, I cleared the table and did the dishes. From her bedroom,

where she bent forward toward the mirror as she applied mascara and lip gloss, she continued to lecture, unable to resist a final word of advice.

"Do I have to tell you about being a good girl? You know what I mean. I don't worry about that too much, at least not yet. But there's always a first time, so don't do anything dumb, not with boys. *Be good.* You know what I mean?"

"*Mother!*" Now I was truly exasperated. "You're gonna miss the bus."

A muffled "Oh, God," a wave of her hand revealing the scarlet of her tapering fingernails, and then she tripped out of the house.

Out of sight, out of mind! I begged the mirror to tell me I was beautiful but it wouldn't cooperate. I pleaded with it to let me grow three inches, promised to settle for two, would gladly accept one. My aunt Mary had told me if only I would go to church and pray, the miracle might happen. I might grow four or five inches, particularly if I lit tall candles.

The building was coming to life. The baby in the apartment across the hall was bawling for his breakfast and would cry for hours before his mother would feed him. Upstairs Mr. Reilly, eighty-seven years old, tapped across the floor with the help of his cane. Tap, brush, tap, brush! It was a wonder that he lived at all, for he had suffered a stroke three years ago and his face and body were twisted.

"I'd rather be dead than ugly," I told the mirror.

But why think of death? It was the first day of school, a new year. Something or someone was waiting for me. Maybe that mysterious Eric or Sven—or a Kenneth or a Gregory—was already on his way to school.

I shut my eyes. "Please, God, let *something* happen!"

One last reassuring glance in the mirror. Then I locked the front door and hurried off to Gilkie High.

Chapter Two

Everyone seemed to be going to school that sparkling September morning. All the ragged kids who had shouted and fought on Lily Street all summer now marched sedately down the street, filled with the importance of their new clothes, their scrubbed faces, their brushed hair. Never again would they look so polished. The clothes would grow grubby, lose buttons, get spotted, get torn, and at the end of the term the Lily Street kids would be as ragged as they'd been all the previous summer. But at the moment they were impressed with themselves, possibly amazed at this first-day-of-school transformation.

For about five minutes I became jealous, wishing I were six years old again, wishing I could remain six forever. It always happened when my mother lectured to me about the future. No matter how I pretended to be blasé, it frightened me. That future, that outside world of which I knew so little, would soon face me, like a big black open mouth. What would I do? I was fit for nothing. It was my mother who had the fantasy about rising to become an executive secretary; I knew I'd never make it as the lowliest stenographer. Oh, God, let me be six again . . . forever six, without a future.

Like everyone else going to high school, I pretended to be bored. Only the freshmen let their excitement show. However, a bright newness vibrated in the air, as if everyone was glad to be back at least that first morning, though of course it would never do to admit it.

"Hi, Cat!"

"Joanna!"

That inimitable whiskey voice had to belong to my cousin, who stood with her five followers, just outside the boundary of the campus. All were heavily made up and all were either smoking or finishing a cigarette. Joanna and her girls formed a clique, possibly the most exclusive clique in the school, and certainly the one most girls would never belong to even if they could. Here there was no mingling with outsiders. The clique enjoyed an undisguised smugness, as if it were a secret society. Clearly they were occupied with something dangerous, shoplifting, I think, but I couldn't be sure.

"Hey, Cat, come on over," Joanna called. Possibly I was the only person outside of the clique that Joanna insisted on being friendly with. I wanted to see my skinny snake-hipped cousin because now as before she held a kind of fascination for me. It wasn't my mother's advice, to which I paid no attention anyway, that made me call back I'd see her later. I had to go to school directly because my fear of the future had been wiped out by a premonition that someone or something new was waiting for me at school. That mysterious blond boy of whom I dreamed? That Eric or Kenneth? What if I were psychic and he were there!

"Catherine. Hey, Cath!"

Before I got to the door three people said hello to me and then Rita Blomberg flew out of the crowd and threw her skinny arms around me. We hugged each other hard and squealed our hellos. Suddenly it was marvelous to be back.

"What's new? Did you have a good summer and why

didn't you call me, Cat? I called you but you were never home. Never."

"I was working at the Mona Lisa. Somehow the summer just went, *pffft,* like that. What'd you do this summer, Rita?"

"Worked. Hey, Cath, you look terrif'," she said, lying.

"You do too. That's a marvelous shirt, that burnt-orangy color. Love it." I was a bigger liar than she. Neither of us were beauties. I'd almost forgotten how *homely* Rita was, myopic eyes behind thick glasses, frizzy reddish hair that reminded me of brillo, and long, thin arms. Yet after the first shock of seeing her, I forgot all about how she *looked,* except for the shirt, which vibrated with color. There was this about Rita: that a certain vitality in her made me feel ten times more alive and awake than I'd been all summer. The crowds were jostling around us, but right away she broke into a serious conversation.

"Catherine d'Amato, artist! We want lots of drawings from you for the *Gilkie Gazette.* At least one a week. We'll feature you. What do you think? I'm associate editor and I'll fight for it. We want the *GG* to be terrific."

"It will be if you're on it. You ought to be editor-in-chief."

"You bet I should and I will be. Don't worry. Carney's the art editor and we both agree we want lots of d'Amato drawings. Besides it'll look impressive in your portfolio."

"What portfolio?"

"The one you'll show when you try to get a scholarship to art school. Time for you to start looking around, Cat."

I laughed. "You're crazy, Rita. Scholarships! Honestly . . . but I'll consult my engagement calendar and my list of commissions and see if I can fit the *Gilkie Gazette* in." I was pretending to be very busy, very important, very affected. A game. She grinned, and then a senior, a boy she knew, placed a hand on her shoulder and pulled her away.

Terrific Rita! She had faith in me, actually believed in me more than I could possibly believe in myself. A scholarship to art school! As if I would dare apply for anything like that. I never dreamed of it. Of course Rita knew all about such things, having figured out long ago where she was going. Lack of money didn't bother her. She had already copped a number of honors—first prizes at essay contests and debating club tournaments, scholarships and grants for one thing or another. She already knew, positively *knew,* that she'd make her way through college and med school and then discover a cure for cancer or something of the sort. For her the future was something certain and radiantly victorious, and she made others feel as if it could be that way for them, too.

"Catherine d'Amato, artist!" Had anyone ever greeted me in such a way? She was so sure of it when I didn't dare to hope.

Above the door of the school, a modern building, was a piece of flashy sculpture with a barely discernible motto carved beneath. "Where there's a will, there's a way," it said. That was Rita. However, the motto remained hidden that morning under new obscene graffiti. The janitor hadn't had the time to scrub it off and most likely he wouldn't bother, so the obscenities would remain while the will and the way would hide beneath the raucous letters, at least for a while.

That first day I would have felt uncomfortable in the crowds that thronged the corridors of the school had not the scene taken on the familiarity of a family reunion. Within the first hour not only had I seen Joanna but other cousins, more distant relatives, and even kids I used to know when we lived on Ravenna Street. The Mariani twins hugged me and then went on. Louise and Paula Cipolli, with whom I used to play jacks, stopped to say hello, and even Tom Bacco, who used to call me "Monkey," gave me a wide grin. A few art students came up to ask which art class I would be taking. I was blossoming with everyone's friendliness. Maybe my mother was right. Maybe these last two years of high school would be my best years. A few people liked me. And it surprised me that I could feel so warmly about them as well.

Yet I kept searching for that new boy, that remarkable Eric or Giles who would change my life and help transform me into the great person I longed to be, that charming, talented Catherine the Great. But though I found a few new faces, none of them belonged to the Eric I craved.

As the day passed, with its harsh mosaic of faces and voices, the corridors took on familiar smells—the odor of too many people, a crushed egg-salad sandwhich, here and there a whiff of garlic, the sweet, lingering fumes of grass, and underlying it all the strong, unpleasant smell of newly waxed floors. The day was only half over and already I'd had enough of school.

Obediently and reluctantly I took a seat in typing class, but no sooner had we begun the first exercise on the grim machine with its unmarked keys than I couldn't breathe and had to leave the room. Can you get asthma from typing? I wondered. After a few minutes, I returned to the room and sat imprisoned in the din of tapping keys, the whining sound of typewriter carriages being pulled back and the dinging of tiny bells. Over this noise the voice of the typing teacher rose to a strained pitch. How was it possible that this was what my mother wanted me to choose for my life's work? How could she, how could she!

As soon as the class was over I fled the room. I turned the corner to rush upstairs to the art room and saw my cousin Anthony coming down.

"Catherine!" his voice rose above the din of the crowd. His green eyes lit up when he saw me and we both pushed and shoved so we could get together. We hugged each other, mindless of the snickers and wisecracks this brought on, for we were cousins, more like a brother and a sister who had not seen each other for some time.

"Cathy, hey, you're good to look at!"

"You too, Tony. What's the latest?"

"I dunno." He grinned. Of course he knew I was referring to an important musical contest which he had recently won. No secrets in the family.

"The *contest,* Tony."

"Contest? What contest? Oh, you mean *that* contest!" he joked modestly, then leaned over to whisper in my ear. "I'll be doing a solo in the spring with the symphony."

"Wonderful! Terrific! I'm so glad for you, Tony. It's the best thing I've heard all day."

We lingered on the stairs while people rushed past us. I'd almost forgotten how good it was to be with Anthony. We might not meet often, but when we did, as on that crowded staircase, it was almost as if we'd been together all along. Why we should be close in a way I wasn't with any of my other cousins except for Joanna was one of the mysteries I did not understand. Each of us wanted for the other to live well, to thrive, and above all to *be;* we came from the same place, we understood that place and each other, we cared. That was it, that we cared for each other. We could have stayed there all day talking, but the bell jolted us into reality.

"I'll see you?" he asked.

"For sure," I answered.

Mr. Everett, lean and refined to the point of being ridiculous in his Norfolk jacket and Brooks Brothers shirt, considering he was teaching an art class at Gilkie High, welcomed me in the confusion of the class. "Ah, here she is,

Catherine di Borgia of the dark paintings!"

Was I supposed to smile? The remark wasn't funny. I stared darkly at Mr. Everett and inwardly groaned at the thought of another year in his class. He liked me well enough and occasionally encouraged me, but I needed a sharper teacher. Without meaning to, I sighed, and one of the most promising art students—big, shy, overgrown Ed Magill— nodded in sympathy. All too often he became the butt of Mr. Everett's jokes, since Mr. Everett simply didn't know what to do with him. Here was this enormous boy, this remarkable draftsman, who quietly went his own way. He devised his own signature, a frog, working it unexpectedly into everything he drew. Had someone in the New York galleries discovered him, critics would have made much of his sardonic comments, but Mr. Everett, never understanding them, disregarded him as if he weren't there.

"Now then, let's get started on this still life!" Mr. Everett said cheerfully that first day of class. He was referring to the arrangement he had set up—a cheap guitar with strings missing, a newspaper, a wine bottle, two wineglasses, a pat-terned tablecloth, and behind them all, a pinned-up drape.

"Wow! Paris, 1910! Just think, Ed, we're about to dis-cover Cubism!" I remarked sarcastically, just out of Mr. Everett's hearing. Ed sighed mournfully, then picked up his conte crayon and I wondered where in this boring setup he would place his melancholy frog.

Then I was back in the halls once more and this time Joanna shoved her way through the hordes to get to me, shrieking, "Cat, hey Cat, wait for me!" I waited and she caught up with me, grinned and posed in what must have been a new outfit, a tight skirt and shirt that opened with five buttons down the front. She would be after something, I was sure.

"I've been thinking of you a lot lately. Did you get the vibes?"

"So that's what they were!"

"Cat, I got something important to talk with you about," she whispered confidentially, interrupting herself as a rough male nine feet high pushed into her. "Hey, who d'you think you're shovin'?"

Her voice came on strong, a make-believe toughness in the tone, but within seconds she was smiling at the gawky senior. She turned toward me again.

A dangerous person, this cousin of mine. But I never wanted to keep away from her, not when we were children and not now. Either it was that low, husky voice of hers, or that fearlessness which made us so different from each other, or simply an unexplained affection that wouldn't let me turn against her. In short, I liked her in spite of myself.

"Can I come over to your house tonight or will your mother be there?"

"She'll be there, Jo."

"Damn. Then somewhere else. Can you meet me at Shookey's Coffee Shop at eight?"

I had an idea of what she would ask and I knew already that my answer would be no, but I agreed to meet her there.

"Great! Don't forget!"

She winked as though we were locked together in a conspiracy and then left me to join her girls. Soon the six of them, Joanna and the Notorious Five, were sauntering down the hall to class in what they must have thought was a seductive walk, all of them but Joanna jiggling in an exaggerated way.

"Aren't they the beauties though!" Rita laughed, coming up and slipping her arm through mine. "You have World Gov, don't you? Let's go together."

We walked toward the distant classroom. "It sounds so

depressing, doesn't it, "World Government." The counselor made me take it."

"Depressing maybe but exciting, too," Rita said. "Blood will run. I'll see to that. The more argument, the better I like it. But I guess you're different, aren't you? You don't like to argue much, do you?"

"No. Maybe I've heard too much arguing. I don't like to fight. A weakness, I suppose. But I'll like watching you You can be such a wildcat, Rita."

"A wildcat yet!" Rita laughed, pleased at the comparison.

"It must be fun to say what you think and be so forceful. I can sit through a class and never give an opinion. It doesn't mean I don't think. I just don't talk about it."

Maybe that's why I liked drawing and painting. That said whatever I wanted to say, better than words. But I was getting depressed, not at the thought of another dull class but because of the fear that this year would be as pointless as last year at school had been.

As we turned the corner of the corridor, we passed a tall girl . . . or was it a teacher? . . . striding vigorously in the opposite direction. At first I had the sensation that this girl or woman was radiating light, but of course that was only an impression, created by the combination of a pale, fine-featured face and a long mane of corn-silk hair tied at the nape of her neck with a salmon-pink scarf.

I turned to watch her disappear, while Rita kept on talking. "Come on, Cathy, it's getting late. We want good seats."

"Rita, do you know who that was who just passed us?"

"About a million people have just passed us."

"This one was different. A blonde girl, maybe a woman. Long hair tied with a scarf."

"Miss Alcott, I'll bet. The new gym teacher. Didn't you know?"

"Know what? All we did in gym today was get our lockers

assigned and listen to a lecture from Dawes about the showers and stuff. Where's Schmidt?"

Miss Schmidt had taught gym forever. She was one of the pillars of Gilkie High, a porky instructor who had barked like an army sergeant at countless gym classes.

"Schmidt's gone, Cath, back to Iowa for some family crisis, and apparently she's going to stay there, so they had to get someone at the very last minute. Nothing like old Schmidt, is she?"

The brief glimpse I'd had of the new gym teacher could not have lasted more than a second or two, yet so intense was the impression she made on me that I could think of nothing else all through class. I had never seen Miss Alcott before and yet she reminded me of someone, but who could that possibly be? Why should she seem so familiar? All through World Government I tried to recall her face and that remarkable stride of hers so I could understand this strange sensation of having seen her before. I got nowhere until the ear-splitting bell at the end of the hour blasted the answer from my subconscious and dashed it out in front of me.

Miss Alcott was the image I had seen all last summer when I stared into the mirror and begged it to change me into someone else.

Chapter Three

The image of the new gym teacher, mostly an impression of light streaking down a dark hall, lingered as I put in my two hours of work at the Mona Lisa after school and into the evening as I sat at dinner with my mother.

"Tell me, how was school?" she asked. Home for the night, she had changed from the murderous black pumps and tight print dress to pink shaggy slippers and a flowered housecoat which made her appear enormous but comfortable.

"Come on, what was it like? New classes, new faces, new friends?" she asked eagerly while I dawdled, spearing a French fry with my fork. It would be important to get her in a good mood because sooner or later I'd have to let her know I wasn't going to follow in her footsteps as a typist. Once more my old tricks would have to save me.

"Well, Mom, it was like this," I said brightly, getting up from the table. That was always how I began my imitations. "Same old Mr. Everett!"

I exaggerated his willowy stance, the slightly affected speech, the prissy way in which he picked up a piece of chalk, and his self-appraisal as he called me his Catherine di Borgia. Then, wiggling as much as I could . . . there not being much to wiggle with . . . I became one of Joanna's girls, chewing gum, looking around flirtatiously. From her I turned to Mrs. Dawes, the ugly fiend in charge of the locker room at gym.

My mother roared. "That's one thing you can do. Imitate. Even as a little girl, you could keep us laughing for hours. You used to do everyone in the family, everyone in the block. Even now, Carol asks me if you do it anymore."

"Just for you, Mom," I said. It was tempting to imitate people and animals . . . I'm not sure why, possibly because I could do it . . . but I was finding out it was cruel, since it was only the weaker qualities that the imitator pounced on, seldom the good ones.

"How's the typing?" my mother asked.

"Fine. Only the class is overcrowded. They may not be able to fit me in."

"But you've got to take it. You tell them that. Insist on it."

"Mom . . ." I began, implying she didn't understand how impossible that was.

She finished the pie on her plate and then rubbed her fingers around her gum where the food got stuck in her bridge. It always sickened me to watch her do it. I bounced up to do the dishes and she helped clean the kitchen, then collapsed in the living room in the one easy chair which held her snug—a safe cocoon, while she watched Merv, Mary, Rhoda, or whoever happened to be on.

It would be another endless evening and I was choking with restlessness. Then I remembered I was supposed to meet Joanna.

"Hey, Mom, I'm going out. Need some notebooks for school."

She didn't turn her head toward me until the commercial came on. Then she said she didn't hear me, so I had to repeat it.

"You're sure that's all you're gonna do?"

"Mom, you've *got* to have notebooks for school."

"Okay. Don't take too long."

She was reabsorbed in the television program as I left.

Joanna was waiting at Shookey's, sitting alone in a corner booth, a cup of black coffee in front of her and a cigarette between her long, tapering fingers. They sparkled with rings —a showy emeraldlike stone, a gold snake ring, a silver ring set with a large turquoise.

"Hi, Cat! I was afraid you wouldn't come," she said as I sat down. "What can I get you? Coffee, a sandwich, some pizza?"

"You sound like my mother," I said. "We already had dinner."

Joanna ordered two coffees from the pale girl who took the order with an indifferent okay. Two toughs swaggered over to the table and began to joke with Joanna. One of them looked me over too thoroughly. In another moment they would have eased into the booth with us.

"Buzz off," Joanna said in a hard voice. "We're talkin' private."

They lingered, but she fixed her cold green eyes on them and they shuffled off reluctantly. If only I were as tough as she!

"What did you want to see me about, Jo?"

She took a long time inhaling, snuffed out the cigarette and then blew out a long stream of smoke, all the while regarding me. Then she spoke, a honeyed quality creeping into the husky voice.

"Cat, you still working at the Mona Lisa?"

I nodded.

"How much money d'you make?"

"Enough. That's my business."

"Sure. It's a great job, sweeping up hair, breathing in hair spray, and all that doggy fetch and carry stuff. 'Oh, Catherine, would ya go out and get me a Coke?' 'Be a good kid and get me some cigarettes too, would ya?' 'Would ya rub my back?' 'Do ya mind changing the baby while I'm having my hair done?' "

"Come off it, Jo," I said, offended at the mocking tone of her voice and uncomfortable because everything she said had been true at one time or another. "Mrs. Russo is really okay. I'm not complaining, so why should you?"

" 'cause I care about you, Cat. I don't like to see you slaving away and wearing those scuzzy clothes. Like that shirt. My God, where'd you get it? Something the Goodwill threw out? What d'you do with all that money you make? Give it to your mother?"

"Let's leave my mother out of it. I do what I want."

The little that I earned was supposed to pay for clothes, drugstore items, and other things I needed, but most of my money went to McVay's Art Supply Store. I was an art supply junkie.

"Cat, get this straight. I wouldn't say a word against your mother, because she took me in when I was a kid, that time when I really needed a place to go. I'll never forget that. But you have to admit she's not exactly easy to live with. It's not easy for you."

"I'm not complaining."

"We have so much in common, Cat," she said sympathetically. "Your mother's not easy to live with and my poor mother . . . God, it's in and out of the hospital all the time. One day she'll go in and won't come out again. She's a walking skeleton."

"I'm sorry. Really, I am."

Nobody in the family knew exactly what was wrong with Joanna's mother, whether it was a slow-growing cancer, bouts of mental instability, or something else. My aunt Frances was such a distant relation, actually a second cousin, that the family could disregard her without feeling too guilty about it. She was seldom invited anywhere and yet she was never completely forgotten, either. Aunt Carol sent her a tiny allowance each month and my mother was forever sending her "a little something," a bottle of cologne or a new night-gown, when Aunt Frances went to the hospital. "After all, she's part of the family and the family stays together," my mother said.

Joanna continued.

"It's not just our mothers that are difficult, Cat. What about our fathers? Gad, it's awful when mine gets out of prison and comes around to see us. It's always such a relief when he gets caught again and has to go back."

"I think mine left for good. We'll probably never see him again."

"It's just as well. I always liked your father, you know, but when I think of what he did to you . . ." Joanna shook her head.

"What do you mean, 'what he did'? What do you know about it?"

"Shhh! Take it easy. You want everyone to hear about it? Everybody knows how he used to be after you all the time until your mother put an end to it. And then how your grandmother got mad at your mother for getting a divorce, but I don't blame your mother at all. We're all on your side."

Furious now, I stood up and flicked off two angry tears. "In the first place, it's none of your business or anyone else's about my father and me. In the second place, you and every-one else are imagining all kinds of things that didn't happen, and in the third place, he's still my father. I'm going home. I didn't come here to talk about that."

Joanna put her hand on my sleeve and pulled me back. I sat down again.

"Take it easy. You're right. It's none of my business, but you know it *is* in the family. Everyone knows everything. No secrets. Catherine, your life could be lots happier than it is and I want to help you."

"You don't have to help me. I'm doing all right," I said.

"But you could do much better. Remember what it was like when we were kids together. What fun! Some of the time. As for the rest . . . remember when my father was arrested and my mother had to go to the hospital in an ambulance? I was all alone and so scared. Then your mother and father came over and took me home. You lived on Ravenna Street then. Remember?"

"Sure."

Joanna had been pale with shock and fright, but pretended it was all a big joke, as if parents went off every day and left a nine-year-old daughter home alone. She sat at the kitchen table while my mother warmed up some dinner for her, and she "laughed" so hard that she had to put her head down on the table. Real tears streamed down her face. That night she curled up in my bed and let me hold her while she wept. For a week I had a sister. We slept together, rubbed each other's backs and told wild, made-up secrets. She whispered my Italian name, Caterina, and I whispered hers, Giovanna. That week, a sad, sweet time of closeness.

Now my cousin broke out of her revery and returned to present time. "See this shirt I'm wearing?" She stroked the well-tailored collar. "Fifty dollars, pure silk. This skirt? Fifty-eight. As for the shoes . . ." She held out a long, slim foot on which a highly styled snakeskin shoe fit smoothly.

"I don't dare tell you how much these cost, but you won't get them by sweeping up hair in a beauty parlor."

"So what?"

"Come in with us, Cat. You saw what I did with the others? Viola used to be a fat piece of grease before I transformed her. The same goes for Edna. Remember what slobby things she used to wear? Today she had on a sixty-dollar dress."

Personally I thought that all of Joanna's girls had a cheap, slutty look about them, no matter what their clothes might cost. Only Joanna possessed a natural style, a cool, elegant quality. The question was, where did the expensive clothes come from? I had an idea but wanted Joanna to tell me.

"Where do you get all this stuff?"

She smiled slowly, secretively, then bent forward to talk in a low whisper. "Confidential, Cat. I guess I can trust you."

"Sure."

"We don't steal. We take what rightfully belongs to us."

"Come again? Isn't that double-talk?"

She lit another cigarette. "Let's look at it this way. It's a kind of sharing. Take our cousins, Gloria, Sue, and Theresa. They go to the most expensive private schools, take riding lessons, wear the best clothes. Do they deserve it more than we do? Are they better than us just because their father is a smart businessman, which really means he's probably crooked, and they've got a pushy mother like Aunt Carol? Are they better than us?"

"Not better. Just luckier. Some people have more than others, that's all. But stealing is wrong. And aren't you afraid of getting caught?"

Joanna smiled in a superior way, as if I were a young child that had to be taught a lesson. "Just how d'you think business or government or banks would make it without lots of stealing? They just use different names for what they do and it sounds all right. What we do is . . . well, we don't pretend, that's all. As for getting caught, you learn ways so it doesn't happen. Vi got taken in once, but they let her off with a lecture. Cat, you're a natural. You got quick fingers and a dreamy, innocent look. Come in with me. I'll teach you. Think of the wardrobe you'll have. And money."

"Money? You steal money?"

"Not directly," she smiled. "We can't keep everything we take, so we turn it in to this guy . . . I can't tell you his name . . . and he gives us cash. You could sure use that, couldn't you?"

"Sure. But, Jo . . . well, I don't know."

Jo took advantage of my hesitation by snapping her fingers and ordering two more coffees. "Cat, I can read people like open books. I *know* you're dyin' for a different kind of life. A better life. Work with me. We get along fine. In a couple years we'll be out of school and maybe we can live together. It doesn't have to be here—maybe New York. Think what that'd be like!"

The earnest green eyes were begging me to say yes and I reconsidered. Of course I wanted to leave Lily Street, and New York would be heaven. As for living with Joanna . . . now as always I was drawn to her, to that smooth olive skin and the elegance of her bony profile. She was the one who had always been sure of herself. If only I had that kind of confidence! Joanna excused herself to get a fresh package of cigarettes and while she was gone, I thought about how it used to be with us, images flooding through my head.

Catherine, seven years old, dallying with Joanna, who is taller, older, and wiser, along Commercial Street. A hot summer day. Crowded streets. Cars honk their horns impatiently as the traffic snarls. Women block the sidewalks as they stand talking,

arms filled with bags of groceries, small children
tugging at their skirts. An old woman in black sits
at a second-story window and watches the street,
knowing who comes, knowing who goes.

The little girls snake their way through the
crowds, then stop at The Garden of Venice, a
restaurant that has been gutted by fire and is being
rebuilt. Ben Piccola, the artist, is standing on a ladder,
painting murals on the wall. A blue canal, gondolas,
striped poles in the water, and palaces. Cupids flying
everywhere. " 'allo, Caterina," he says to Catherine,
" 'allo, you Mariucca," to Joanna.

"I'm not Mariucca," she says. "Hey, can we watch
you paint?"

"Be my guest."

Catherine could stand there all day, mouth open
with wonder as he paints, but Joanna is easily bored.

"Hey, Mr. Piccola, can I put the little you-know-
whats on the cupids, huh? Would you let me? Just
one."

Mr. Piccola does not know whether to be amused
or angry at this outrageous request from such a little
girl and he settles for a scolding. "You should be
ashamed, a little girl like you thinking about such
things."

Catherine hangs her head down and blushes with
embarrassment, but Joanna does not know what
shame is. "Aw rats, let's go," she says in a voice that
is low and husky, even then.

Prieto's fruit-and-vegetable market stands on the
corner, a happy violence of colors, fruits arranged in
boxes and cartons taking up half the sidewalk,
bunches of bananas hanging from the ceiling of the

store. Catherine, greedy, wants to taste everything—
nectarines, peaches, grapes, figs, pomegranates, most
of all the pomegranate, so round, so red. To hold it
in her hands, to sink her teeth into it . . .

"That's what you want, the pomegranate?" Joanna
whispers, then talks out loud. "Hey, Mr. Prieto, you
wanna see Catherine make a monkey? She's real
good." Catherine blushes modestly.

"Let her do it, she's such a cute little girl," four
women customers beg Mr. Prieto. He softens, gives
in. Always ready for an audience, Catherine becomes
a monkey, pulls the usual antics, pretends to climb
the pole that holds up the awning, peels an imaginary flea from her side, her armpit, her hair, and
examines it closely. The women roar. Mr. Prieto
smiles.

"She's good, Joe. Give her a real banana."

Catherine thanks him and shares it with Joanna as
they walk away. Joanna leads her up a side street
and draws her into the hallway of an apartment
house. They carefully avoid a pile of dog droppings.

"See, I told you I'd get one for you. Here!" Joanna
dangles a huge pomegranate in front of Catherine's
eyes and shows another which she has taken for
herself. Where she managed to hide them when she
is pencil thin and wears only the briefest of faded
dresses, Catherine cannot imagine.

"Here, take it, Cat."

"You stole it. You're not supposed to steal."

"I didn't *steal* it, silly. I borrowed it, that's all."

Joanna is eating her pomegranate and red juice
runs down her chin. Catherine tries the tempting
fruit, puts it in her mouth, but cannot accept it there.

She places it back into her cousin's hand and Joanna
puts her arm around her shoulder.

"Don't tell, huh? It's a secret. *Our* secret," Joanna
says, on the verge of threatening Catherine.

"I gotta go home," Catherine says, slipping out of
Joanna's grasp. She will not give her cousin away.
Besides, everyone steals fruit, but she cannot. Is
there something wrong with her?

At home on Ravenna Street, Aunt Mary is visiting
and helping her sister make fettucini. Catherine's
big brother, Vince, is wearing a new baseball suit and
shows it off proudly. Aunt Carol walks in with her
daughters and Catherine plays with Gloria, Theresa,
and Sue. Dolls, clothes, tea parties, little girl games.
The kitchen is filled with talking and laughter. But
Catherine does not breathe a word about what
Joanna has done. Maybe, if she tries hard, she will be
able to forget it.

Joanna returned to the table and I returned to the present
—Shookey's on a warm September night.

"Cat, want a piece of pie? It's good. I'll treat."

"No thanks, I'm not worried about paying," I said, and
to prove it I picked up the bill the waitress had left.

"Now that's silly," Joanna said, her eyes narrowing
through the smoke. At that moment she could have passed
for thirty or more. "Cat, I know what you're going through.
Get wise to yourself. Come in with me. I'll help you."

"No, it wouldn't work. I'm no good that way."

"You don't know until you try. It's not just money I'm
talking about. It's a whole way of living. You could be
beautiful, but you don't know it. I could train you. I could
make you gorgeous in every way."

It could have been the answer to what I wanted so much,

to *become* someone else, but I couldn't do it. Besides I knew, positively *knew,* that if anyone were going to get caught it would be me.

"Thanks a lot, Jo, but it's not for me."

"Okay. We're still friends, aren't we, Cat?"

"Sure, Joanna."

She left a tip larger than the bill I paid, and then we walked out into the warm, sweet night. The evening was leaving a sorry taste in my mouth. Joanna was more like a sister than anyone I'd ever known, but I feared we were growing farther and farther apart. Then she said something that startled me, so close it was to the truth I'd never told anyone.

"Cat," she said casually, "did you ever wish you weren't part of the family? I mean, you know, how they fight, how everybody knows what everybody else is doing. The way Aunt Carol is forever boasting about Gloria. The way some of the uncles are sort of loud. Let's say you could begin life again and be anything you want. Would you want to be Catherine d'Amato?"

"What a question!" I said. It's what I'd been thinking all summer, but I could not easily admit it. "I really don't know."

She smiled, knowing she had scored a bull's-eye. If I were so content with being myself, then why did I choose to see a tall, slender, confident Catherine in the mirror? Why did I long to leave Lily Street and move away where there wasn't any family? Why did I so often wish my mother were someone else?

Joanna peered into my eyes and grinned slowly and wisely like a cat.

"You wouldn't be the first to want to break away. Think about it. Any time you want to change your mind, come to me, Cat. Be seein' you."

With that she walked away, leaving me even more uneasy

and confused than I had been before. I started for Lily
Street, then remembered in time that I was supposed to be
buying notebooks, so I stopped at the drugstore before
hurrying home.

Chapter Four

A t ten-thirty, gym class. I hurried to the locker room to change into the regulation gym suit of harsh blue cotton, tennis shoes, and socks. The locker room had built up a strong aroma of sweat and rotting gym shoes, a smell the empty summer could not dissipate. Voices babbled and re-verberated from the walls, the usual raves and groans about va-cations, mock despair over homework, whispers and outbursts of laughter about boys. Last year I had achieved a brief pop-ularity—if such a word is not too strong—when I was urged to imitate the bellowing Miss Schmidt, an act which had to be done with someone watching to see that she wasn't approaching. The girls giggled, told me I had her down perfect, and for a little while I came to life for them. But now, removed from the giggling and sociability, I became used to the fact that I was little more than part of a silent background. Would I have wanted to be one of those other girls for whom life seemed to be one endless giggle? No, not them.

Joanna and her girls moved lazily into the locker room after the bell rang and changed into their gym clothes as reluctantly as possible; it was part of their style that they never hurried. I avoided Joanna. I wanted to rush upstairs to the gym, yet hesitated, fearing that Miss Alcott might turn out to be ordinary after all and that first startling glimpse of her the day before only an illusion of light.

At first I could not find her because of all the girls in that overcrowded class, and then I discovered her in the far corner of the gym, where she frowned over a book of class lists. Possibly she was less tall than she had appeared the day before, which comforted me a little since I feel strange with people who are too tall. It was her long legs and supple slenderness which suggested a few inches she did not actually have. Impressed by the way she held herself, the back straight and the chest pulled up, I wondered if she were a dancer. The blue leotard and tights that she wore added to this impression, but even more so was the grace with which she bent over to catch a paper that fell from her class book. Her features were fine, possibly too sharp and intense, her nose slightly pointed, and yet everything about her was palely golden, the deep-set blue eyes a striking accent. The Indian summer sunlight that poured through the tall, narrow gym windows illuminated the long, ashen hair which had been pulled severely to the crown of her head and from there released in a flow of pale gold.

Right away I wanted to draw her.

She glanced at her watch, put down the class book and picked up a drumhead which she began to beat with a padded stick. The drumhead looked like a tambourine without the metal pieces which would have made it jingle. A few girls stared at the new teacher, but the others went right on talking. The gym buzzed. Miss Schmidt would have blasted our ears with a shrill whistle, but Miss Alcott, walking to the center of the gym and beating continuously, catching as many eyes as possible with her own cool glance, eventually caught everyone's attention.

"Good morning," she said. "When you hear the beat, it means that class is beginning. I expect you to be here at that time, ten-thirty-five, and you are to be absolutely silent and ready to work. I believe in promptness. All right, we'll begin. Let's make a big circle and please sit down."

Her voice surprised us with its dry coolness, its self-confidence, its detachment. It placed an invisible wall around her, a force field through which we dared not try to pass. Even that army sergeant, Miss Schmidt, a hundred and seventy pounds of blubber, whose voice had bellowed like a distraught bull, had somehow been less forbidding. Slowly the girls formed a vague circle. I could see them exchanging glances that asked what kind of a person this was they had to deal with. Let her be good, please, I prayed, wanting her perfect in every way.

"That circle is ragged, too bunched over there, too spread out here. Let's make it a pure, even beautiful, circle. I want each of you to have a vision of a circle in your mind and see yourself as part of that perfect circle."

"Huh?" Nobody had ever talked to us in this way, not at Gilkie High. Did Miss Alcott speak with an accent? At first I couldn't define it because there was nothing foreign about it, and then it came to me, it was the accent of the rich, the educated, the highly refined. I'd heard it in movies on television, but even if I hadn't, I would have recognized it vaguely as such. Whoever she was, one thing was certain: never "one of us," she had wandered into Gilkie land a stranger, a foreigner.

We rounded out the circle.

"Thanks, girls. That's much better." She rewarded us with an unexpected smile so sunny that it won back some of the girls who had already turned away from her. "Now then, this is third period. My name is Miss Alcott. And now, before we begin to work, I'll check off your names to see if you're all here."

Her reading of the class roll was disastrous, for she could not pronounce any name that was not "typically" American, that is, English or Irish. Perhaps I do her an injustice. Yet she stuttered over certain Armenian names, could not tell the -steins from the -steens, and crippled the Italian and Spanish names.

"Please make sure I'm pronouncing your names correctly," she said after stumbling over Ajemian and Rodriguez. I expected she would call "d'Amato" as though it rhymed with *tomato* with a hard "a," which was often the way it sounded when certain teachers said it, but she made an even worse bungle of it, so that a titter of giggles broke out. Her face reddened and I felt guilty for having a name she could not pronounce.

She tried again and got closer: "Catherine dam-a-toe."

My muffled "Here" could not be heard, and it was Joanna who shouted out the corrected pronunciation, which led to a slight confusion as to who Catherine d'Amato was. Finally I raised my hand, embarrassed for having been the subject of a small scene, which was one way of getting off to an unfortunate start with a new teacher.

"All right, girls," she said in an earnest voice, still remote but not unpleasant, once she had finished the roll call. "This class will probably be unlike other gym classes you have known. Our approach will be different. We'll be thinking about ourselves differently. Now we've all been given good, workable bodies, but it's obvious that we abuse them. So we're going to look at ourselves honestly—I warn you, this will not always be easy but it's necessary—and then we're going to ask ourselves what we need to do in order to make the most of what we have. I expect you will find yourselves growing, changing, and becoming aware of yourselves in a way that may be entirely new."

Some of the girls scowled. What was she talking about?

"Hey, Miss Alcott, ain't we gonna play basketball and all that?"

"Yeah. Miss Schmidt let us have a regular volleyball team. We didn't do nothin' about our inner selves and all that. We jus' played volleyball."

A muttering of protests made her stiffen and I felt sorry for her. Some girls had the reputation of baiting new teachers and substitutes until they resigned and it was possible they were planning to give Miss Alcott a hard time. But she smiled and nodded at each aggressive complaint.

"Of course we're going to have games. Basketball, of course! Maybe we'll have a team. Volleyball. Soccer. Tennis in the spring. And gymnastics, too. I hope we'll have a few Olgas and Nadias among you. I want to see lots of activity here!"

The dissidents were quieted temporarily. She received a small murmur of approval and some applause.

"*However,* you need an incredible amount of work. Look at the way most of you are sitting, backs bent, stomachs out. Whatever you do, basketball, soccer, anything, you must get into condition and that's what we'll work on first. So let's begin. Up now, everyone. Quickly. On your feet. Let's stretch up, up, up! Pretend there's a piece of fruit up there on a branch, a red apple just out of reach and you want it. Stretch, stretch, stretch up!"

She demonstrated and we followed. I could practically see that imaginary apple just out of reach, a red apple in the middle of the air. If I could reach it, I'd grow taller, two inches, three, maybe more. Could it happen through mere suggestion? Now we stretched forward, backs straight, first to one side, then to the other, always pushing further than we thought we could go. The beat of the tom-tom and the cool directive voice worked us mercilessly without rest for twenty-five minutes of exercise. We became winded. We perspired. And what was our reward? A scolding.

"None of you are working hard enough," she said as we collapsed. "You must learn to concentrate, to center your every thought on what you are doing. Forget everything else. When you stretch, your mind should be stretching, too. All right? Any questions? I'll be expecting improvement as we go along."

We didn't know how to take this woman who came to teach us. Her remote voice, her unexpected smiles, and above all the intensity with which she worked herself and made us work differed from that of any teacher we had known. We had hardly caught our breath when she herded us into the north corner of the gym.

"Now then, I want to see you walk, from that corner to the one diagonally opposite. No hesitation now. With each beat of the drum, a new girl will start."

Who would have thought it was so difficult to walk across the floor? Even the boldest girls became vulnerable, embarrassed as they walked alone. For me it had the quality of a nightmare in which I have to perform naked in front of an audience. Miss Alcott judged us silently except for an occasional inadvertent sigh. A strut, a glide, a rapid scurrying, a defiant bragging stride, a self-conscious funereal crawl— only two girls walked well, Linda Holmes, who had studied ballet, and my cousin, Joanna, who moved sensuously with a self-confident pace, neither too fast nor too slow. However, her five girls brought on uninhibited laughter and sarcastic applause. Viola d'Amore, stripped of her shoplifted elegance, shimmied across the floor in an unusually baggy gym suit;

Edna Doughty dipped into each step; Joey, the fat girl, walked carefully as though the floor were made of eggs; and the last two, Marcia Delaney and a red-haired, heavy-busted girl named Greta, placed one foot in front of the other voluptuously like the burlesque queens in old movies. Everyone laughed; even I had to cup my hand in front of my mouth.

Miss Alcott, angry, pounded a fierce drumbeat. "We'll have nobody laughing at any performer. No comments. Most of you should be blushing with shame. I've never seen such a pitiful demonstration of a simple walk. Only two girls among you walked with any dignity."

A low grumble began once more but Miss Alcott held up her hands for silence. Once more that unexpected radiant smile burst on us.

"Well, I know it's not easy to walk across a floor, not the first time. But by the end of the term, possibly before, all of you will stride like beautiful self-assured young women and you'll be proud of yourselves and I'll be proud of you, too. All right, let's end with a game of Follow the Leader. I'll lead you today, but in the future, each of you will become the leader. All right, everyone in a line. Let's walk proud and tall on tiptoes. Walk, walk, walk, walk, walk!"

The tom-tom became her voice as we followed her first in a large circle, then in random curves. The beat slowed down and as we lessened our pace, it became difficult to keep our balance. She doubled the pace, tripled it, and soon had us walking so fast it was harder than running. Slowing down again, we walked in a crouch, moved backward, walked on all fours, straightened up, skipped and kicked our way with high, sideward kicks. We trotted, ran, and finally leaped around and around the gym until the walls swam in circles and I thought my lungs would burst. A number of girls dropped out, but I stayed until the end, announced by three triumphant beats on the tom-tom which coincided with the first bell.

Exhilarated, I stood trying to catch my breath and holding on to my side where a small pain was stabbing. Even so I experienced a strange emotion; I was happy, simply happy. But not everybody was pleased.

"Miss Alcott, when're we gonna play basketball? Miss Schmidt used to start us . . ." one of the less enchanted girls complained but Miss Alcott cut her short.

"For the last time, I want you to know that I am not Miss Schmidt and my classes will not resemble hers. When you're ready for basketball, we'll play basketball.

"Let me give you a word of warning. I am something like a cat. Stroke me in the right direction and we'll get along, but rub my fur the wrong way and you'd better watch out. Do you understand? Good. Everyone shower, please. I'll see you tomorrow."

The bell released us and we scattered, running pell-mell down the stairs to the locker room to see who'd get to the showers first. Would Miss Alcott last? A few girls liked her, a few could not stand her, and most were indifferent or puzzled, for we had never met anyone like her before. Complaints came from the showers. "If only old Schmidty was back . . ."

"Hey," someone said, turning to me. "You're the one who used to imitate her. You were so good at it, I'll bet you can do Alcott."

A few girls came over to watch. They wanted a good laugh but they wouldn't get it from me. "I'm sorry; I just can't do her," I explained.

But as I stood under the steaming shower and let the water pelt me with burning heat and chill me with icy cold, I determined that's just what I would do, imitate Miss Alcott. I'd learn to stand erect as a tree, to walk with pride, and to move sinuously and gracefully like a cat. I would learn to speak clearly and not muffle my words and mumble the way I did most of the time. My smile would be dazzling, not the vapid, flirtatious grinning my aunt, my mother, and Mrs. Rossi thought I should adopt, but a genuine, sun-filled, triumphant smile. Eventually I would grow taller, I would surely walk straighter, and possibly I would become beautiful.

Whatever physical freedom I'd gained in one short hour with Miss Alcott was undone by a few minutes in typing class. My shoulders grew tense, my back stiffened, and I could not breathe.

If I could take gym for two hours instead of one, how much healthier I'd feel. As for typing, I could take that in summer school.

Instead of going to the Mona Lisa directly after school, I went to the gym. Mrs. Dawes, the woman who managed the locker room, blocked me in the hall with undisguised hatred. I wasn't being singled out. A true democrat, she hated everyone. Maybe if I'd spent most of my life in a locker room, I'd find it difficult to love anyone.

"You there! What d'you want?"

"I have to see Miss Alcott."

"What about?"

"When I see her, I'll tell her," I said with unexpected courage. She squinted, not trusting me, but finally gestured toward the gym.

"In there," she said.

I slipped through the door quietly and stood there. Miss Alcott was practicing what I took to be dance movements, although they weren't like any dancing I'd ever seen before.

She was circling around slowly and sinking toward the floor, head buried in her arms. From that position she rose quickly, arms thrust high and chest out as she balanced on one foot while the other leg moved slowly upward and out to the side. She held this difficult stance for a long time, then broke into a galloping movement around the floor in a circle, from time to time stopping to experiment with a break in the pattern. She moved with the grace of an animal when it thinks it's alone.

Then she stopped and glared at me, suddenly aware of my presence. A tiny frown of annoyance broke the smoothness of her high forehead.

"Yes, did you want something?" Unsmiling remoteness.

Embarrassed, I mumbled apologies. "I didn't mean to interrupt you."

"Yes. Well, what do you want?" She softened but I could see she was impatient, waiting for me to leave.

"I'd like to take another gym class."

"Instead of the one you're assigned to, you mean?"

"No. I take third period gym and I want to take fourth period gym, too, instead of typing."

"Two gym classes? Well, what about that!" she said, her voice still cool. She walked to the end of the room where she kept the class register and brought it over to where I stood. As she leafed through it, I watched her and realized she was not as young as I first thought. Twenty-eight? Thirty, maybe? Something old like that.

"Let's see. What's your name again?"

It was disappointing to me that she didn't remember. "I guess there's room for you. You'll have to bring in permission slips and all that. It's all right with me if you're sure you really want *two* classes?"

"Yes, I'm sure. I do. Thanks very much," I said too intensely, as if she had given me a gift.

Later that afternoon, as I pushed the broom across the floor of the Mona Lisa Salon of Beauty, I pretended I was Miss Alcott. I moved in a calm, dignified way.

"Something wrong? You look funny. Don't you feel well?" Mrs. Russo asked.

I could not tell her I was being Miss Alcott. I only smiled in a superior sort of way and forgave her her ignorance.

Chapter Five

On Saturday it was the family again! Aunt Mary had phoned me and after a long preamble on how was mother, how was I, how was school, she came to the point.

"Catherine, I was wondering, could you come over and finish the drawing of Mickey? It's George's birthday next Friday and I'll want to get Mickey's picture framed with the others."

"Right! I didn't forget, Aunt Mary. I'll be over first thing Saturday morning, before work."

During the summer I had had my first art commission when Aunt Mary asked me to do some portraits of her children as a birthday present for her husband. *Commission* is too proud a word, and in the end I didn't accept the money anyway, because a milkman's wife with five children has a hard time of it. It was my love for Aunt Mary that induced me to go there and sit for hours making pastel drawings of each child while Aunt Mary clasped her hands in admiration. Only Mickey had been so rebellious about posing that I wanted to do his portrait again.

I was glad to do it—heaven knows I really love my aunt

Mary and I like my uncle George too—but as I climbed the stairs to the top floor of the three-story tenement where they lived, it occurred to me that the family was hemming in my life. Whatever I did mattered only as far as the family approved or disapproved of it; the family defined my boundaries. Now I was becoming aware of a world beyond that was possibly more fascinating, but this thought was yet too vague to be put into words. It had something to do with Miss Alcott, I thought.

As I walked into the kitchen, I barely escaped being run over by Mickey riding by on a small plastic motorcycle which pushed me back into a line of freshly washed diapers. Aunt Mary apologized.

"It looked like rain today, so I hung them in the kitchen."

Aunt Mary was holding the baby in her arms and in spite of an incipient mustache, her face wore the sweet expression that could be found on the Madonnas pictured on the calendars that covered the kitchen walls. She could never bear to throw away anything with a picture of a Madonna or a saint on it. The breakfast dishes were piled in the sink. Were there only five children? It seemed like fifteen. Josie was hitting her little sister, who wailed; Mickey, making *vroom-vroom* noises on his motorcycle, tried to run everyone down; Joey stood picking his nose; and the baby spit up on Aunt Mary's shoulder. Aunt Mary smiled serenely through it all. Oh, God, I thought, I'm never going to get married. Never.

"Catherine, all the drawings are so beautiful. I love them, even Mickey's. It's a shame you have to do it over again."

"I'd better do it again." Mickey had made funny faces all through the first sitting and I hadn't caught his likeness.

"Well, he promised to be a good boy today, didn't you, Mickey? He's going to sit real still, aren't you, honey?"

While I took out my sketchbook and pastels, Aunt Mary bribed Mickey to abandon his motorcycle and sit on a kitchen chair in front of me, and then gave him a lollipop. Try getting a likeness of a four-year-old licking an outsize lollipop! Aunt Mary stood in back of me, watching as I drew, chattering the whole time.

"Catherine, you always had the gift. Remember when you were a tiny little thing and you made drawings on every page of the telephone book?"

"Yeah. My mother spanked me with the book."

"You were so cute. Remember when you lived on Ravenna Street and you drew what you called 'fancy ladies' all over the walls. Each one of them had a dog on a leash."

"My mother wasn't crazy about that, either. You were so sweet, Aunt Mary, buying me my first sketchbook."

"It was only a cheap thing. Newsprint. A newsprint pad."

"It was a wonderful gift. I was so proud of it."

Since then, how many sketchbooks did I fill? A hundred? More? A sketchbook became an appendage like an arm or a leg. I couldn't exist without one. But was I really talented? Did I have a true gift or did I only like to think so? Lately I'd been growing fussy; my drawings were never good enough. Yet there was no question that I would keep on drawing.

Mickey was giving me a hard time that morning. While Aunt Mary talked about the past when we all lived on Ravenna Street, Mickey placed the wet lollipop on his motorcycle and insisted on showing me how he could stand on his head. Aunt Mary didn't notice.

"You were so good at imitations. Your father would take you to the zoo and when you came home, you could do all the animals. Especially the monkeys."

"Monkey, make a monkey!" Josie cried, and Mickey joined the chorus, begging for the imitation. A good bargaining point.

"Okay, Mickey, if you sit still for eight minutes without

your lollipop, I'll do a monkey for you."

It worked. He sat with only a few twitches, some scratching and experimental eye-rolling, and I finished the drawing. Then, true to my word, I hopped about like a monkey, mugged, searched for imaginary fleas, and exhausted my monkey tricks. The children loved it.

"That drawing is beautiful, simply beautiful," Aunt Mary said. "George will be so happy with it. Now I've got some coffee for us, and cookies. They're store cookies, but good."

I accepted the coffee but said no thanks to the cookies, since I'd seen Joey, the nose-picker, fingering each one. Aunt Mary sat at the table with me and leaned forward confidentially, ready for a little chat.

"I'll tell you a secret, Catherine, 'cause I know you can keep mum. We're gonna have another baby. It's in the oven right now."

"Really!" That was hardly a surprise since Aunt Mary always appeared vaguely pregnant, whether she was or not. Briefly I thought of Miss Alcott's slender figure and decided I'd rather have that than babies, a new thought, as I'd always taken for granted that of course I'd do what was expected— grow up, get married, and have children.

"Are you happy about it, Aunt Mary?"

Her hesitation told the truth. Her eyes lowered, then flickered as she answered. "Of course I'm happy about it. Each child is a blessing from God."

Almost immediately again her moon face shone with serenity. Of the three sisters, she was the youngest, the most religious, and the most old-fashioned. Her answer was exactly what anyone might have expected.

"I wish my mother felt that way about me, that I was a blessing," I said.

"Why, your mother loves you, Catherine. I'm sure of it."

"I'm not so sure, Aunt Mary. I'm in her way. Who wants a sixteen-year-old kid around when you're looking for another husband?"

"Your mother's life isn't easy, but I know that she loves you. You must believe it. Catherine, do you go to church?"

"Once in a while," I said. Actually, almost never.

"Do you go every day? Every week at least? You should, Catherine. It's such a comfort. You need God. Joey, stop picking your nose."

Hoping she wouldn't carry on about it all morning, I changed the subject.

"Aunt Mary, would you mind if I did a drawing just for myself? I'd like to draw you and the baby."

"Like this?" she shrieked. "But I'm a mess. The baby spit up, my hair's undone . . ."

"It's not a photograph. I love it, just the way you are. If the kids wouldn't mind posing just for a little while, that would be neat, too."

I moved to the far corner of the kitchen to get some distance while the children, all of them jumping around and trying to elbow each other out, clustered around their mother. This was my first drawing of a family group, something new for me, an involved composition marked by a repetition of shining, dark eyes and thick, dark hair. I had to work fast, for the baby was pulling strands of Aunt Mary's hair from the bun she wore in back, Josie was whining, and little Bianca simply walked away. Still I caught them, captured them forever with my pencil. I concentrated for a minute more on Aunt Mary's tired patient smile and then she begged my pardon while she rushed to the stove, where a pot of soup was about to boil over.

"That's beautiful," she said about the drawing, but she would have been rapturous about any scribble I made. She tried to press a ten-dollar bill in my hand and then fought with me when I wouldn't let her stuff it in my purse. At last she gave up, insisted on giving me a bag of cookies, made each child dampen me with a wet, mushy good-bye kiss. Then I skipped down the shabby back staircase and ran to catch the bus.

One minute I knew the genuine happiness of having finished the portraits and knowing they weren't too bad; and the drawing of Aunt Mary and the kids, which, though sketchy, felt right. The next minute I was biting my tongue, for the bus crawled, which meant I'd be late for my job at the Mona Lisa Salon of Beauty, and I hate being late. Mrs. Russo would scold. She always smiled when she scolded, not because she tried to be nice, but because frowning brings on wrinkles; the anger would be there in her voice and then I would have to apologize because jobs were hard to find, especially for sixteen-year-olds. Besides I was *obliged* to be a good worker because it was Aunt Carol who had persuaded her friend Mary Russo to take me on.

I didn't wait for the bus to get to the salon but jumped off two blocks early and ran the rest of the way.

"Catherine! Five minutes late," Mrs. Russo greeted me. A hundred eyes centered on me—the beauticians, the customers, some with their shampooed heads and others who sat baking under the driers, magazines in their laps.

"The bus was slow. I'll stay later, okay?" I asked in a low voice and without waiting for an answer hurried to the back of the shop to change into my green uniform, an ugly nylon dress, the smallest size available but still too big for me.

First I picked up the pushbroom and swept up the hair from the floor. Then I polished the mirrors, washed combs, counted out curlers, arranged magazines, and ran over to the drugstore for cigarettes, Cokes, or whatever anyone wanted. Mrs. Russo had recently trusted me to take down appointments over the telephone when everyone was busy, for the shop hummed with "regulars" during the day and an increasing number of girls and women from the insurance companies and the factories after hours. The hairdressers slipped all the tips into their pockets and I saw nothing of them. It was my job to remain anonymous, yet I didn't mind. My hands performed their tasks; my dreams remained my own.

Dreams. Vague glimpses into another world. All during the summer I had developed my visions of that certain Eric or Kenneth, someone handsome yet faceless, walking with me through the park, taking me to a disco, or better yet, speeding along the highway on a motorcycle while I clung to his back. Now that Eric or Kenneth faded while I polished my fantasies about Miss Alcott. How I wanted to be like her!

"Look at 'er. Dreamin' about her boyfriend, I betcha," a stout customer yelled above the roar of the driers as Olga, the best hairdresser, pulled the curlers out of her hair. Immediately all the "cows" turned to grin at me.

"Catherine," Olga asked. "Mrs. Hoskins wants to know when you're gonna let us trim your hair."

My eyes flashed bullets at Mrs. Hoskins while Olga combed out the thin wisps of her graying hair. My mop of dark curls, which would never quiet down into the long, sleek hair I craved, never ceased to frustrate me, but I didn't have the courage to cut this unmanageable jungle of hair. Surprisingly Mrs. Russo came to my rescue.

"When Catherine is ready to have her hair cut, then she'll have it cut," she said severely enough to put Mrs. Hoskins in her place but not so firmly that she would lose a customer. A few seconds later she put her hand on my shoulder, pulled me toward the back, where we wouldn't be heard, and spoke to me in a confidential voice.

"Really, Catherine, when are you going to do something about it? Don't you want to get yourself a boyfriend? I'll cut it for you without charge anytime. Style it. A part on the side, a shoulder-length cut. Maybe we can straighten it a little. You'd be darling, simply darling."

"Thanks, I'll let you know when I'm ready," I said. Her kindness wasn't lost on me, but she was beginning to sound too much like my mother, who wanted me to wear my hair like my cousin Gloria.

Another customer, possibly trying to make up for Mrs. Hoskins, asked me if I still did imitations. "One time last year I saw you doing some and you were great. You oughtta go on the stage."

Still another customer begged me to do something, as she hadn't seen me, and another woman swore that she had and I was sensational. Mrs. Russo nodded to me to go ahead, and I didn't mind at all. Every head in the salon looked toward me now, waiting. I took a deep breath and then began, a mishmash of imitations—TV personalities, including Colombo, Charo, and the girl who did the weather reports on the local station; a particularly eccentric English teacher at school who fastidiously clung to her southern accent; and finally some of Joanna's brassy girls. I was careful not to mention any names. Success! The women laughed; even the hairdressers smiled and murmured what talent I had and why didn't I go on the stage. The day lightened. Compliments flew and I bowed and thanked them and went on washing dirty combs.

When I left the Mona Lisa at five, the Indian summer day was still glowing, the sun turning the trees to lime green and deep yellow on their journey to scarlet and gold. A bittersweet time of the year.

I let myself into the apartment, for my mother would be out shopping and wouldn't get home until after nine. She had left me a TV dinner, whose gloriously painted wrapping bore no resemblance to the corpselike mound of frozen stuff inside. Leaving it, I found crackers, poured a glass of orange

juice for myself and sat on the front stoop to watch the sun
bathe the old brick houses across the street in shades of cerise
and orange. Kids were playing ball in the street, a crap game
was in progress in one front yard, and three old ladies
weighed down with bags of groceries lumbered along the
sidewalks. A small girl chanted as she bounced a ball and
circled a thin leg over it on every fourth count, something I
used to do.

Suddenly without warning a strange sadness and longing
came over me and I didn't know why. I had enjoyed the
exaggerated praise of Aunt Mary that morning and the applause of the women in the salon, but I didn't want to spend
my life imitating someone else. I wanted to be a personage
myself, someone that even Miss Alcott would one day applaud. Oh, the brashness of that thought! My desires were
vague, having something to do with wanting to move away
from Lily Street, wanting to be more than simply a member
of the family, of wanting to *become,* but what I would become, I could not tell, not yet.

Chapter Six

Gradually, through ceaseless daydreaming, I devised a world in which I wanted to live, a Karen Alcott world. While I passed my days in the bleak Lily Street apartment with its stained brown walls, the crowded school through which I moved mechanically, and the ironically named Salon of Beauty where I worked anonymously two hours every day after school and most of Saturday, at the same time I was discovering "the other world" that was miles and miles from "the real world."

Far away from "sunny Italy" lay a land of vast cool skies and snowy mountains, a place from which Miss Alcott came, spiritually speaking. Actually she was extremely American, of a very old American family, she happened to tell us one day—an odd bit of information from one who chose to remain so reserved—but her spirit, so it seemed to me, was undeniably northern, possibly from Alaska, the far north of Canada, Finland, Norway, or Sweden. A winter world of ice so frozen that it burned at the core and a summer world of long nights brilliant with the Aurora Borealis, the northern lights. A place of fire and ice.

One afternoon on my way home from the Mona Lisa, I

saw a poster of the harbor of a small coastal town with great silent peaks in the background, the few houses painted red with high-peaked roofs, a northern place. I begged the travel agent in whose window the poster was displayed to sell it to me. She couldn't do that, she said, but found a somewhat battered copy of the same poster, told me this town was on the far northern coast of Norway, and it was unusual that I liked it so much. I hung the poster on my bedroom wall, a symbol of the intense quietness for which I longed.

At dinner that night my mother scolded me. "Since when don't you like spaghetti? And with clam sauce, too. *Vongole con maccheroni,* your favorite. And not cheap, either. You know how much these clams cost? And you sit there. You don't touch them."

"I'm sorry, Mom. I know it's good, but I can't eat it."

"What do you mean, you can't eat it?" I shuddered, expecting a storm as she stood solidly, hands on hips, and glared.

"I have to give up pasta. No olive oil anymore. Just plain salad. In school they told me I have to lose weight. About ten pounds."

"You lose weight? My god, if you were any skinnier, you'd slide under the door."

"But I'm not skinny. Look!" I got up and pulled my jeans tight over my stomach to show the curve that seemed to me to bulge monstrously. I wanted my front flat so that my hipbones would stand out like Miss Alcott's.

"Catherine, that's nothing, not a stomach at all. It's normal to have curves. That's what boys like, what men like. Cath, you got to eat something. You can die of starvation, do you know that? My sister Mary told me the story about a girl who . . ."

And so on. My mother's stories were always about a foolish girl who did what I was about to do and, whatever it was, died because of it. Even so I passed up the spaghetti for a boiled egg, a touch of salad, and a cup of tea. I even said no to the Snowpuffs my mother had brought home for dessert, four pastries in fluted white papers, cakes covered with a layer of red jelly, sprinkled with coconut, and topped with a fluting of whipped cream with a cherry in the middle. My mother worked her way through one while drinking coffee from a chipped cup.

"Am I ever tired," she confided. "Carol sure has it easy and even Mary can stay home all day. Sometimes I almost think it wouldn't be so bad to be one of the cows. . . ."

The "cows" were the married women who stayed home while their husbands worked, brought home the money, took care of the bills, fixed the plumbing when it didn't function, and brought their wives presents of perfume, roses, or candy. My poor mother! She detested the cows at the same time that she longed to be one of them. Time after time she swore there wasn't a man you could trust, yet she wanted nothing more than to be married again.

"If I weren't here, I'll bet you'd find another husband," I said, wanting her to admit it, but she wouldn't.

"It's nothing to do with you, darling. All the good men are taken," she replied pessimistically.

Yet every time Aunt Carol or Aunt Mary called to tell my mother they had found "the perfect man" for her, she went hopefully to meet him. During the previous spring Aunt Carol had found the man she called Mr. Right. Good-looking, barely forty, generous, refined, single, well set in a good job. What more could one ask? My mother left me alone frequently in order to go out with him. I loved the growing joy that swelled within her as she went out with him to dinner, the movies, an occasional dance, baseball games, which bored her although she pretended to be excited by them, and parties where she met his friends and family. After four

months of this, my mother invited him home for "a little
Italian dinner," something she gave the impression of having
tossed off, although she had worked for two days over the
home made ravioli, the gnocchi, and a remarkable ricotta
cake. When he appeared at the door, a bouquet of roses in
his arms for her, she introduced me.

"Oh," he said softly. "I didn't know you had a daughter."

After that he phoned once or twice, but he never took my
mother out again. It was clearly my existence that ended the
love affair where he was concerned. But even if my mother
wished I'd never have been born, she never so much as
hinted so. I mustn't ever think I was to blame, she insisted.

"How's the typing class?" my mother asked as we cleared
the table.

"It didn't work out. Too many kids in the classes already.
Don't worry, Mom. I'll take it in summer school."

"Catherine! Why don't you listen to me? You've got to
take it if you want a decent job. And you're going to *need*
it," she said, her voice shaking with anxiety. It would be best
to calm her down.

"I know, Mom, but *don't worry.* I can take it in summer
and I'll take shorthand, too. You'll see."

"You're just like your father, full of promises, full of
baloney, too. He was always about to do something wonderful, get a new job, patent an invention. Did he ever do it?
Ha! I couldn't trust him. Now I can't trust you. What will
happen to you?"

She poured another cup of coffee for herself and slumped
in her chair, lips curved down. My father was a loser. My
brother, Vince, was lost, too. My mother must have considered herself a loser because she wasn't married. And now
apparently I was going to follow right along with a double
inheritance of losership.

The doorbell rang. I pushed the buzzer, then waited for the knock.

"Vinnie!"

My mother sprang from the table, threw her arms around him in an embrace and pulled him toward her.

"Hey, Ma! How are you? That's some death grip you've got," he laughed, liking the attention she gave him.

"Where've you been, Vinnie? My God, you're so thin. Concave. Come in, I got dinner for you. Spaghetti and clam sauce. Remember how I used to make it for you?"

I could have cried for Vincent, for his paleness, his unkempt hair, the cheap striped sweater he wore under a half-torn navy peacoat and the crocheted cap that stuck to the back of his head. My mother scolded him, cried a little, and hugged him again. His presence brought her to life and ended all the weariness she'd brought home with her. She chatted, fussed about the kitchen, asked a hundred questions and told him he mustn't go until she mended his peacoat and darned the hole in his sweater. Where was he living now and did he have a job?

I could have told her all this myself, since Joanna, who knows everything about everybody, kept me posted on how he sometimes worked at a pool hall, now and then appeared at the greyhound race track, and occasionally acted as delivery boy for a small florist shop. He came home only when he was broke and I didn't have to guess that he would walk away from Lily Street that night with ten, twenty, or maybe forty dollars in his pocket.

Vincent and I exchanged simple greetings, nothing more than a distant how-are-you-but-don't-tell-me-please sort of hello. Then I begged to be excused to do some homework for a big test the next day.

I closed the bedroom door and threw myself across the

bed. Vincent could break my heart because even now I could not forget Ravenna Street on those days when it was less than paradise. My father's voice still echoed in my ears as he shook Vince, then a little boy, by the shoulders.

"You dumb kid, you stupid! You'll never be anything but a stupid no-good!"

Don't say that, I wanted to cry. I hated my father for those ugly words, that heartless prophecy. But they were the very ones my mother had shouted to him. And so the endless cycle had produced the Vincent he predicted. Where did it begin? Had my mother's parents spoken to her like that? Had my father heard it when he was a child? Would Vincent carry on that crippling tradition if he had children? Losers all. Losers to come.

What about me? Lying on the bed in the dark, I fingered the cheap bedspread idly and wondered if what Joanna had said was true. It was. If I'd had my choice I would have been born to any other family but this. There, it was out. That was the truth.

In the kitchen my mother was begging Vincent to have another helping of spaghetti, to finish the other Snowpuff, to wait a minute and she would make espresso for him. From his laughing protests I knew she must be flirting with him, hugging him, and hovering over him.

Let her have him then, I thought bitterly. I'd leave the both of them in a minute. But where would I go?

The image of Karen Alcott swam before me. I was seeing her less as a teacher than as a dancer, an artist, and a priestess. If only she were that, a priestess, I would serve her in every way I could, become her servant, her neophyte. She would train me so that I would become like her, growing tall and serene. I would not dress as a servant but as a dancer with leotards and long skirts like hers. During the day I would be an artist, a painter. At night I'd be her friend, her companion. We would go out together into the world, to a thousand exciting places, to meet artists and dancers and writers. We would believe in each other. I would go with her anywhere at any time and would do whatever she wished.

All she had to do was say, "Come, Catherine!" and I'd leave my mother and family forever.

Chapter Seven

"Good morning, everyone! Let's make a perfect circle. Proud backs. Heads high. Some of you are doing better but you're slumping, over there. You too. Straighten up. That's better. I have something to tell you today, something important." Miss Alcott beamed. Only a few cynical groans followed this announcement.

It was three weeks after school had begun and the Indian summer had given way to true autumn, with the wind taunting the leaves from the few trees that I passed on my way from Lily Street to school. The sun, less brilliant now, often hid behind the gray clouds of fall, already foreboding the winter. In other years the fading of the sun had filled me with sadness but right now my heart was so light it no longer mattered that the gray coldness of winter would soon be on its way. I had Miss Alcott to thank for this new feeling.

She must have been miraculous in at least one way, for nobody had ever detested gym more than C. d'Amato, but now I rushed to each of my classes every day to stretch, to run, to practice balances, and to learn those gymnastics which had always frightened me before. I still ended breathless after each session and it never ceased to hurt, but I would rather have died than have given up on any exercise Miss Alcott gave us.

Her manner became kinder although she was still insistent that we "follow our disciplines." One minute's tardiness meant three running laps around the gym floor. Everyone did every exercise. If we talked, she fixed a steady eye on us. "You cannot divide yourselves by talking *and* exercising." That was sure to be followed by a challenge which hardly permitted us to breathe, let alone talk.

Yet for all that she smiled more, as if she were trying to win over the girls in her classes. She transformed exercises into dance steps, accompanying them less with the tom-tom and more with records. She surprised everyone by playing recordings of the latest popular music, mingled with vigorous Latin dances and exciting drum and percussion discs from Africa. She won over a number of anti-gym girls in this way but at least half the class was beyond reach and would not respond to anything given to them by any teacher. Much of the grumbling ceased.

It was unlikely, though, that she would ever be popular with everyone. She still impressed us as being a stranger, someone different from us, different from all the other teachers. Whether they were liked, disliked, or simply endured, they represented a familiar world; we knew where they came from and what they were like. Miss Alcott was not and never would be "one of us."

And I loved her for it!

If only she knew how much I admired her! But I might have been invisible, for she never glanced my way, never said a word. Still, I was learning patience. One day she would "discover" me.

On that Friday morning, as a few girls sat with straight backs and the rest of us slumped, she spoke to us with more warmth than usual.

"What I'd like to see in this school is the establishment of a modern dance club. I've been watching you and believe that some of you would do very well and would enjoy it. First, do you all know what modern dance is?"

A babble of answers. A few girls thought it was ballet, a few more had studied it elsewhere, some confused it with disco, and most were not interested.

"All right. Let me explain. It's not ballroom or disco dancing, which is what you do for your own pleasure; it's something like ballet in that it's performed before an audience. We've been doing exercises and preparations for it all along, so whether you realize it or not, you're already acquainted with it. In Dance Club we'll work intensively on technique and compose dances. I'm hoping to get started so that we can take part in the Christmas concert and manage a complete program in the spring."

So this is what she really wants, I was thinking. She would train us, whip us into shape, teach us dances, make us good enough to perform. Us? I was already seeing myself as part of the group. A few girls who obviously admired Miss Alcott were asking questions but others slouched, bored and disinterested.

"Hey, Miss Alcott, when are we gonna have basketball?"

"Yeah. Can't we have a team instead of this modern dance thing?"

"Miss Alcott, I'd rather have advanced gymnastics. You promised . . ."

Miss Alcott appeared discouraged but brightened almost immediately. "We're swinging into the basketball season now. Of course we'll have a team and we can have Dance Club, too. As for advanced gymnastics, I have plans; just be patient. Now then, we'll have tryouts for Dance Club a week from today after school. If you have leotards and tights, wear them. By the way, you may wear them to gym if you like.

Next week we'll talk basketball. Any questions?"

That day I asked Mrs. Russo for an advance in my salary, something I'd never done before. After work I went downtown, bought plum-colored tights and a leotard and put them on as soon as I got home.

"Look, Mom, I'm a dancer!" I cried, posing in front of the mirror.

"You're just throwing out your money," she said.

"I don't care," I retorted. Wait till she sees me in Dance Club, I was thinking, performing on the stage, being applauded. Not for a second did I doubt that I would be part of the group.

Setting a regimen of daily practice for myself, I bent, stretched, balanced, jumped, kicked, and turned. I could almost touch my head to the floor in those thigh-splitting floor stretches, something I'd never been able to do before.

She would be sure to demand improvisations in the tryouts and it was there I would do best. In the confinement of my tiny bedroom, I experimented with rhythms and movements, creating the beginnings of a dance. The more I practiced, the easier it was to imagine myself in the group. How close we would become as we worked together. For the first time in my life I would belong to a club.

At the tryouts on the following Friday after school, only thirty-four girls competed for the fifteen places in the club, a sure disappointment for Miss Alcott. But those who tried were so promising! I grew more and more discouraged as I watched the other contestants walk, run, leap and improvise as Miss Alcott directed, for most of those girls had studied ballet and moved with a grace that came from long practice. Miss Alcott announced my name with the same impartial coolness she had pronounced the other names. I crossed my heart and did my best. Afterward several girls told me that my improvisations were "really something."

"You're gonna make it, for sure!" one of them said.

"You really think so?" I asked, eager to pick up any crumb of hope.

During the tryouts, Miss Alcott had appraised each candidate silently and thanked her. When we were finished, she announced that our names would be listed and placed on the bulletin board outside the gym on Tuesday morning.

How would I ever be able to wait so long? I knew I would make the club. It would be the beginning of something new in my life.

Centuries passed until the following Tuesday when the candidates crowded around the bulletin board to see who had passed. I ran my finger up and down the list three times. Could there have been a mistake? Fifteen names were listed, but none of them was Catherine d'Amato.

I blinked back the instant tears of disappointment. Later, perhaps, I'd take this defeat with grace, but at the moment the pain of rejection was too great to bear. The happiness of the last week escaped at once, hissing out, like a punctured balloon.

Chapter Eight

"There you go again, d'Amato. Black, black, black! Is it the color of your heart or is it that time of the month?"

For that I gave Mr. Everett the black look he deserved, a cursing look, but he only grinned. Someday someone would report him and I wouldn't care if they fired him or not, if only a better teacher would take his place. Still, I knew that he liked me and gave me the only good grades I ever got, always an *A* in art.

"Catherine, why are you so obsessed with darkness?" he asked, kindly now, as he pulled up a stool and sat beside me. Was I "obsessed"? When a drawing begins to move, the hand goes faster and the litho crayon becomes more and more dense. Is that obsession?

"Now then, let's take a good look at the model," he said. A student in a bathing suit sat shivering with goose flesh in a hard-backed chair beside a classroom table. The assignment was to draw her against an appropriate background, such as a beach scene or a swimming pool, Mr. Everett suggested, as if we went to the beach or the swimming pool every day! What I saw was a skinny girl with a face that was pretty in a common sort of way. I drew her more or less faceless, centered, alone against an angry cross-hatching of lines that suggested imprisoning walls.

"Your drawing is so *morbid,* Catherine. Yes, *morbid,*" Mr. Everett said, drawing out the word as if he thought it was great. "The model is a nice girl, not a tragic figure. Let's see what Betty's done. Betty, would you mind bringing over your drawing?"

His voice lightened as he called over his pet, a slightly rounded blond girl who obviously worshipped him. She bustled about her desk and brought the drawing, smiling a superior, buttery smile. Betty had transformed the model into a heavily eyelashed beauty, reclining on a chair against a background of flat, blue lake, purple mountains, and turquoise skies on which pasted fluffs of cotton represented clouds. Could Mr. Everett actually admire that drawing or was it so absurd that it amused him? I tried to find the twinkle in his eye and failed. It must have been Betty who blinded him.

"There, Catherine, and what do you think about that drawing?"

"Vomity," I was going to answer but did not dare. Without thinking, I held my nose as if the drawing smelled bad.

He held the work in front of him at arm's length, cocked his head to one side and answered. "Ah, d'Amato, that's the response I would have expected from you. Betty, dear, it's very nice work. Very neat. Very clean."

He gave the drawing back to Betty, who made a face at me and returned to her seat. Mr. Everett leaned toward me and spoke confidentially, quietly. In spite of myself I was feeling sorry for him, for his receding hairline and that dry, slightly disappointed expression on his face. He used to talk to us about Yale Art School (which he may have attended for a summer, probably not more). During my first year of high school, I had the impression he would not be staying long at Gilkie High, for he had a career to follow. Yet here he was two years later, apparently resigned to it. His tweed jacket and Brooks Brothers shirt were showing wear.

"Now, Catherine, when you draw, you should be yourself, not Giacometti, which this drawing resembles, not Picasso, not Matisse, just yourself."

"But, Mr. Everett, I don't try to draw like anyone else. This is me."

"You need control. Everything is too black, too depressing. Remember what Rembrandt once said, that you need a gleam of light in the shadows and a touch of dark in the light areas."

"Okay, Mr. Everett. I understand that. It's really terrific to think that way. I'll try, I really will. But I do see things dark, not blue lakes and cotton skies like Betty. When I look at that model, the crayon tells me what to say; she's all hemmed in, almost as if she were in prison. Not a literal prison. Just caught in some way. Trapped. Helpless."

"Is she the one who's trapped and hemmed in or is it you? Hmm? Catherine, think about it. I mean it. Think about it," he said, raising one finger as if to show that he was the teacher and he was right. In this case he was. Then he moved away.

I bit the end of my litho pencil and stared at the dismal autumn rain outside. His last statement hit me like a stone thrown at my forehead, a piece of hard truth, even profound truth. My drawings were always black, except for the portraits of Aunt Mary's kids and three quick studies I had made of Miss Alcott, which were light arabesques, moving swiftly across the page.

Mr. Everett was sharper than I'd expected. It *was* myself I was drawing, not the model, darkly enclosed in a self-made prison. How I pitied myself as I stared out of the window. I couldn't dance, couldn't draw, couldn't even type—not that I cared about that last thing—couldn't even have begun to make it as one of Joanna's shoplifting girls. How would I ever leave Lily Street? What would happen to me a year from June when I graduated and was thrown into the world? I tried to find the spot of "light in the dark areas" that Mr. Everett talked about, but I couldn't find it. It wasn't there. Then why go on?

I let my pencil wander over a new sheet of paper. It hesitated, scrawled a few lines slowly and then, gathering momentum, curved and flew faster, deeper and darker until at last a face emerged from the scrawls. I could have sworn it had been hiding there in the blank paper, waiting for my pencil to reveal it. A disturbing head, a death mask, it glared out darkly.

My God, I thought as the bell rang, that's my father!

Is it possible that an offhand drawing can warn of things to come? Three days later I had reason to believe it.

The November twilight was coming on in deep swashes of violet and blue and I was home alone. My mother had phoned me at the Mona Lisa, telling me she'd be late and that I was to put a low flame under a half-cooked beef stew and not let it burn. "I got a little present for you too, darling, but you'll have to wait and see what it is!" she teased. That was my mother at her good-humored best, her voice taking on a rich honeyed timbre. She'd come home singing.

The stew barely bubbled on a low flame and the table was set. Having changed to jeans and a faded blue sweatshirt, I sat alone in the living room and watched the deepening twilight soften the room, giving it unexpected mysteries. I liked it that way, peaceful in its silence and dusky shadows. To have turned on the lights would only prove once more that this room with its dismal wallpaper and ill-matched collection of scarred furniture could only be considered ugly, even by the most charitable standards.

The buzzer jangled its unpleasant sound and I released the front door, expecting my mother to barge in. Instead a timid knock announced someone else and I opened the door.

My father! There stood my father, cap in hand, under the one naked light bulb that lit the hall. After four years of absence he came back, a solid ghost. As if this were a nightmare, I wanted to scream but could make no sound.

"Well, Catherine, aren't you going to ask me in?"

"Why, sure. Of course. Come on in. I was just surprised, that's all."

He closed the door behind him and stood silently and awkwardly, waiting. Should I embrace him? After all, he was my father. Yet the last time I saw him, it was in this very room when he was somewhat drunk, when he was chasing me, when he had just caught me . . .

"It's all right, Catherine. You don't have to be afraid of me." His voice, not pleading, only expressed a sad patience.

"I'm not afraid," I answered quickly with a nervous laugh, as if such a thought were ridiculous. "Please sit down."

Nervously I turned on a floor lamp and a table lamp, as if the light would protect me, while he sat, prim and stiff, on a straight-backed chair, a visitor. He glanced at me, then looked around the room.

"So you've still got that three-legged table. I'll bet it still wobbles. And a new television? Very fancy. Color, eh? Same old sofa with the stuffing coming out. And the easy chair, ugly as ever. Your mother's throne. I'd almost forgotten."

The small talk covered an awkward silence. From time to time he glanced at me, then turned away again. Was I too homely or was he too shy to stare? I too was shy, but took in what I could, the way he sat neatly in his bulky corduroy jacket, the dark, curly hair from which I suppose my own frizzy mop had come, though his was neatly cropped, and the hand that held his cap with its long, tapering fingers; those, curiously enough, I had not inherited, my own being short, stubby and strong. Now I remembered how meticulous he had been about such details as his fingernails and the way his shirts were laundered and the quietness of his voice when he wasn't drunk. Traits of a gentleman. Such things I had forgotten because when my mother talked of him, it was only the vicious things she remembered.

Memories flooded my head. Even I could not erase the time he had grabbed her favorite piece of pottery, an Italian bowl with a filigree of porcelain roses around it. He was about to smash it to the floor, but changed his mind and spit into it instead and thundered, "Family, family, family, your lousy family! You think they own the world? They think they own me, but they never will. Never!" Frightened, I had cowered in the corner, but I also remembered that just before this scene, my mother had pecked away at my father, criticizing him until she drew blood, his temper. Would I never forget those fights that sent me fleeing from the house with my hands over my ears!

Now, in the silence of this meeting, I began to understand my father for the first time. To a charming young man who had never had a family to care for him, the Martini clan must have appeared as a stroke of good luck, but once married he must have regretted it. Never would he make enough money to please them, nor would he be sociable enough to attend the unending family parties to which my mother insisted that he go. He fought with her too about going to church. So long as he worked for my uncle Enrico in his liquor store, he stayed within the graces of the family, but when the Italian section was razed and Uncle Enrico moved to Rochester and did not invite my father to go with him, my father could not seem to hold on to other jobs. Too much of a dreamer, my mother said, spitting out the word with scorn.

Suddenly I wanted to tell my father that I understood him and didn't blame him for anything. Would that be unfaithful to my mother? In a way she too was right; the things he had done were not easy to forgive. In spite of a deep desire to forget what happened, I still saw too clearly, as if it had just happened, the last time we were together in this very room in the deepening twilight. At first he had wooed me, his speech slurred because he was slightly drunk.

"Come on, Catherine, come and sit on Daddy's lap."

I had hung back. Then he became abusive, ordering me to come. "Damn it, come here. I'm your father."

The rest was nightmare, his chasing me, stumbling over the coffee table, grabbing my leg, myself screaming and screaming, and at last my mother rushing in. . . . Now there was only silence except for the stew bubbling on the kitchen stove. I turned on more lamps, the pink china-base ceramic lamp my mother had bought on sale in a drugstore and the pole lamp that stood near the sofa, as if each light were a beacon, a message to my mother to come home and save me again. None of this escaped my father.

"Catherine, I tell you, you don't have to be afraid. I only came to see you again. You're pretty. Growing up."

"I'm not growing very fast. I'm sixteen now."

"I hadn't forgotten."

The quietness of his voice gave my father back to me, my father telling me stories at bedtime or chatting as we played cards in the kitchen. Still that last dreadful night would not go away. My mother had flung open the door and found me nearly hysterical while my father tried to explain that he was innocent and hadn't hurt me. She called the police and they took him away. It was awful, the endless questioning at the station and the face of the examining magistrate peering closely into mine, insisting over and over that I tell the truth. My father wasn't arrested after all, but was ordered to stay away. My mother filed for divorce and after that he disappeared, simply vanished, as if he had dropped off the earth.

"Where are you living, Dad? What are you doing now?"

"I'm working here and there, New Haven, Meriden, Bridgeport. Worked on a few construction jobs, took a stint with a landscape firm, drove a truck for an Italian import store. A good job until I had an accident. Put me out of commission for a while."

"I'm sorry. Were you badly hurt?"

"Mostly my back. Couple ribs. I'm mending."

"I hope so." And what more could I say? Better to change the subject. "Geez, I forgot to offer you anything. A cup of tea?" I couldn't bring myself to offer him wine or another drink. "I know. What about some stew?"

"Now that would be great. It smells real good. I don't want to rob you. Just a little. Thanks, Catherine."

More memories as he sat on one side of the room and I stood against the opposite wall. At night when he thought I was asleep, he would spread an extra blanket over me to keep out the cold. It was he who could never stand the harsh northern winters; what a sweetness to care for me on cold nights! And those trips to the zoo where we fed popcorn to the monkeys; a vague sensation of his strong, warm hand holding mine. All these things were making me remember that I had loved him fiercely then and now I ached, we were so far apart.

"I think the stew's ready. Let me get some for you," I said, ducking into the kitchen. As I put the meal together on a tray, a good dinner of brown stew, thick slices of Italian bread, butter, and a cup of instant coffee, I wondered if possibly my father wanted to come back. He would be forty-five now, for he was nine years older than my mother. But I could see the beginnings of an old man in him while my mother could appear no older than thirty when she was in the mood.

"Thanks, Catherine. This is a feast. I'll say one thing for your mother: when she took it into her head to cook, there was nobody better. She was great with the plants too, could make anything grow."

He tried to eat slowly, but once he began he could not stop, nor did he lift his eyes from the bowl of stew until he finished. It's not easy to hide hunger, I was thinking, and wondered if he had been fired from a job or if he'd been out of work for a long time. His despair was saturating the room. He rubbed a piece of bread around the last bit of gravy, then glanced up at me.

"You'll make a man a good wife someday, Catherine. You got a boyfriend?"

"Not really. The boys don't like me much."

His eyes narrowed. "But you like them, don't you? Don't worry. They'll come around in time."

"Maybe. I'm not worried. Dad, did you ever get married again?"

"No. Once was enough. Sometimes I have a housekeeper, you might say . . . nothing much." He dabbed his mouth with the napkin. "You know, Cathy, if you ever want to come down, I could meet you at the bus station and take you out to dinner. You wouldn't have to be afraid, you know."

"I wouldn't be afraid. Thanks for asking. Maybe someday I'll come."

A pair of lies. We both knew I'd never visit him. This first meeting was painfully stiff; the thought of trying it again was unthinkable.

He was finishing his coffee when the door burst open and my mother stepped in. Her arms were full of packages and she was wearing the fake fur coat which at first glance made her appear prosperous, or nearly so.

"Hey, Cath, you should see . . ." she stopped short as she discovered my father. Her packages dropped to the floor. He placed the dinner tray carefully on the rickety table and stood up.

"What do you think you're doing here?" My heart beat rapidly with an old fear at the leaden, threatening voice.

"Well, what's the idea? What are you doing here?"

"Nothing, Bea. Don't get upset now. I happened to be in town and I wanted to see the children. That's all. And I wondered how you were. It's been a long time."

"The kids are fine and I'm fine too, so thanks for your concern. Here's the door. You remember what the judge said."

"Come off it, Bea. I've kept away all this time."

"This visit isn't 'keeping away.' "

"Mom," I pleaded. "It's okay. Really. He just wanted to say hello."

"Keep out of this, Catherine," she said.

As my father put on his jacket, I could see that it was badly worn and he moved stiffly and slowly—not yet recovered from the accident, I supposed—but my mother stood rigid and unmoved. Couldn't she see that he was broken now and she didn't have to be afraid?

"Good-bye, Catherine, and thanks. You're a nice girl," he said to me, then turned to my mother. "Good-bye, Bea. Better find someone to take care of you while you're still good-looking and not too old yet."

His eyes moved slowly around the room once more, as if he were trying to memorize it so that he could hold on to it forever. Suddenly I ran over to him and threw my arms around him. He kissed me warmly, a fatherly kiss. Then he turned and left, closing the door behind him.

When the outside door clicked shut, my mother, still

breathing deeply with anger, faced me. "What's the matter with you, Catherine, letting him in like that? Did he touch you? Did he chase you? Did you forget what happened before?"

"Of course not. Did you look at him, Mother? Can't you see he's old. And hungry. And broken. Besides, he's still my father. Nothing will ever change that."

"Don't shout at me like that," she screamed then pursed her lips tight. She picked up her packages and spoke more quietly. "Catherine, you're very young and you're soft-hearted, like a young girl. When you're older, you'll understand these things."

"I understand them now," I screamed and ran into the bedroom, slamming the door. I was hating her, hating everything about her. I wanted to stick a knife in her fat belly, but all I could do was lie there and weep.

Whose fault was it? Hers because she nagged him or his because he was too weak to stand up to her? All I knew was that I was tired of it all; I had always been tired of it, and I wished I'd been born to another family, a different family miles away. But I would be forever tied to them, my father and my mother, and there was no escape. Except one, the final one, but I shuddered to think of it.

My mother was bustling about the kitchen as though nothing had happened.

"Come on, Cathy, stop moping. Come and have dinner."

"Don't want any."

"Sure you do. You'll feel better when you have something to eat. Besides, I got a present for you."

"I don't care!" I shouted. What good was any of it, dinner, a gift, an evening of television. I didn't want to be Catherine d'Amato anymore. I'd had enough. I beat the pillow in anger and then fell asleep.

At nine o'clock my mother woke me, wooing me with

kindness and good sense. "Come, Catherine. It won't do you any good to go on like this and it's not making me feel any better. It's too bad about your father. Don't you think I feel sorry for him? Anyway, he's gone and we're left and we have to make the best of it. Right?"

"I suppose."

I ate the heated-over stew without tasting it. My mother deliberately talked about everything but my father.

"And here's a gift, made especially for you," she said with forced cheerfulness. I opened the box and took out the red sweater she had bought for me, instantly detesting its harsh finish and ruffled collar. Thanking her with as much enthusiasm as I could muster, I put it on to please her. Damn, couldn't she do anything right? Once again I saw myself a loser like my father and like my mother, too.

"There, it's terrific, beautiful, just your color!" she said. "And now I want you to forget about what happened today. Smile a little, huh? There's a good comedy hour on the TV tonight and I want you to watch it with me. It will cheer you up."

"All right."

She settled into the cocoon chair and let herself get swallowed up in the big bright screen, but my father's presence lingered in the room. All through the comedy hour, with its peals of canned laughter, tears kept rising in my eyes no matter how furiously I brushed them away.

Chapter Nine

November. The skies were silent, drained of color. The air itself was frozen but the snow had not yet come—a cheerless time of year and the perfect setting for my growing depression. Twice a day I saw Miss Alcott in class. She acknowledged every other girl in the class but never noticed me at all. More and more I began to feel like a big nothing. I wondered, did I exist?

Mrs. Russo asked me to work even longer hours on Saturday, since she was enlarging the Mona Lisa. Sometimes I longed to get out. Anywhere. I thought of visiting my grandparents, who lived in the country beyond Canton, in the same farmhouse in which they began their life in America when they came over from southern Italy years ago. Once I had lived with them when I was very small and every time I saw them I felt a rush of love for them. Then I'd forget them again; they were so old and so old-fashioned, still immigrants, still talking Italian most of the time. We used to visit them but ever since my mother divorced my father, feelings between her and her parents had been so strained that we never went there anymore.

Still the restlessness persisted, so one Sunday I hiked out into the freezing countryside just outside the city and watched the crows fly out over the stubbled fields.

At school the next day, I was aware of a certain hushed whispering in the halls, but I didn't know what was wrong. Fortunately I ran into Joanna on her way to the girls' room to sneak a smoke. She always knew everything.

"Jo, is something wrong? Everyone is so quiet."

"Don't you ever know anything, Cat? Ed Magill committed suicide this weekend. On Saturday. Cut his throat." She demonstrated this graphically with one finger and a rolling of her eyes.

The blood drained from my head, leaving me feeling faint and ill.

"Tell me you're kidding me. I can't believe it. Saw him just last Friday. Are you sure?"

"Yup. Didn't you see the paper yesterday? There was a whole story about it."

"What did it say? Why would he do something as awful as that? Jo, he was so nice. Never said anything against anyone. And he was so good and funny and shy."

"I know. From what the paper said, nobody ever spoke to him. He wrote a note—get this—saying he hoped he would not be too much trouble. The thing is he must have planned it for a long time. He returned all his library books, cleaned his room, left a list of possessions that were to go to different people, and you know what else he did? The final touch: he earned two hundred dollars and left it to pay for his own funeral."

"I can't believe it. I can't believe it," I moaned.

All that day Ed Magill haunted me, Ed with his big, burly body, the broad, open face too big for the wire-rimmed glasses that seemed too small, as if they'd been made for a child. Now that I thought of it, I had always been aware of Ed; I said hello to him when I saw him and I praised his drawings; he had more real talent than anyone. But I never really talked to him because he always seemed part of the scenery, the fellow who walked alone along the edge of the corridor as he went from class to class.

I was guilty then, for thinking only of myself, as guilty as everyone else.

Mr. Everett must have also felt guilty, for he was pale, spoke little, and somehow acted as frozen as I felt. At least he recognized Ed's talent, but he couldn't understand Ed's fearless uniqueness and it angered him, all those frogs and toads and weird creatures, until finally he paid no attention to Ed at all, just as if Ed weren't there. On the day we drew the model in the bathing suit, Ed drew most beautifully a girl far lovelier than the model, but he gave her the face of a frog. In everything he did there was always that creature, either drawn large or tucked away in a corner like a signature. Once he had made a print, a drawing of a toad, and the glistening eyes looked out so imploringly, I was moved in a way I couldn't explain. I told Ed I loved it, and he gave me a print, which I hung on my bedroom wall. But why did it take me so long to realize that this was Ed's self-portrait and the eyes that begged for understanding were his?

"I exist too," the frog said. "Can't you see that? I'm alive."

If Mr. Everett couldn't understand this, perhaps he shouldn't be blamed. He didn't have the vision to see what the drawings said.

"Now, Magill," he had said. "What the hell is that all about? Can't you do anything without those ugly beasts popping up all over the place? You think you're funny, do you?"

"No, not really," Ed had said meekly.

"Well, you drive me up the wall. You'll never be an artist. Never in this world."

"But he is an artist! He is now and he'll be a great one someday. He's got vision!" That's what I thought, that's what I should have shouted, but on the day that conversation took place I was too fogged-in by my own problems. So it was a sin of omission. That which I should have done, I did not do and now it was too late.

All that Monday after the event, I heard wisps of talk. "He was so nice."

"It's funny, he was so big and yet you never noticed him somehow."

"Nobody ever said hello to him. All the people in this school and nobody ever said hello to him. That's what the paper said."

For once I forgot about Miss Alcott. Ed filled my mind. Like everyone else I bore the responsibility for his death.

"Jo, will you go to the funeral with me? I've never been to a Protestant funeral."

She agreed. We both found something somber to wear, although her black blouse was too provocative and not in the least mournful. I had to make her button it up.

Together we took the bus to the funeral home, a colonial red-brick building with white trim and a red canopy that stretched out over the sidewalk. Very fancy. An organ was playing mournful hymns as we walked in and I hoped I wouldn't cry too much. It's embarrassing to be such a weeper. Ed's mother, a large woman with a run in her stocking, sat in the front row and at the sight of her wiping her eyes and of the small man beside her, probably Ed's father, staring ahead dry-eyed, my eyes filled. I would never last it out. The chapel was crowded with kids from school, some curious and others possibly regretful, like me.

The minister droned on with a sermon so dreary and in-appropriate to Ed, whom he probably didn't even know, that I lost all inclination to weep, but then I melted when eight members of the Glee Club, standing straight, shining, and reverent, sang a song for Ed. It was Tony playing "Ave Maria" on his violin that sent the tears pouring down my cheeks and I used up all my Kleenex and had to poke Joanna and ask her to lend me some. The chapel, crowded though it was, became hushed. The minister asked for a long, silent prayer, and then it was time to go, to file past the open coffin.

"I'm not sure I want to," I whispered to Joanna.

"C'mon, you gotta. It's not so bad," she assured me.

We waited in line while Ed, who had remained unnoticed in life, was now on view for everyone to see. All those who had never smiled at him, never acknowledged in any way that he was alive, now paid tribute to him.

He did not appear as ghastly as my imagination portrayed, with deep red gashes and remains of blood. The undertaker had rouged his cheeks too much but had had the good sense to let him wear the pitiful wire-rimmed glasses which were so much a part of him. He appeared to be sleeping in his best suit.

What I was not prepared for was the sense of peace that surrounded him. A peace that nobody alive would ever have. Long after Joanna and I escaped outside to the raw, rasping November wind, the words printed on the ribbon that wound around the bouquet at the foot of his coffin kept repeating themselves in my mind, fresh and new, as though I'd never heard them a thousand times before: REST IN PEACE.

With that a door opened for me, a possible way out of

my own life, a life that promised nothing, far less than Ed's. To rest in peace, what more could anyone want? Possibly death wasn't the worst thing in the world after all. I'd have to think about it.

Chapter Ten

It was time for something good to happen to me now. Something new, a surprise, something very good. After Ed's funeral the English teacher said in class, in the blurry self-righteous manner I had fun imitating before, that literature teaches us that though life is full of darkness, it is also full of light and that it all balances. Something like that. I never quite listened, but that was the drift. All right, I knew now something different had to happen in my life.

About a week later, Joanna was wearing an outfit that couldn't be ignored.

"Wow, Joanna! You going to a night club or to gym?"

"D'you like it?" She smiled, pleased with herself, blowing a huge bubble of gum.

Only she could appear like a gypsy and get away with it. A purple cotton dress with a low, gathered neckline and swinging skirt cut in tiers. On her long, narrow feet were outrageous red espadrilles with long ribbons that criss-crossed up her slender legs. Her hair was held back with two small combs covered with plastic fruit and flowers, all of it an extravagance.

Beside her I was more drab than ever. What was the mat-

ter with me that I went around looking so dull. A leftover
from a rummage sale. My own fault. Gloria's clothes hung
in my closet and I wouldn't wear them out of pride. All right,
I'd try something else. New clothes. Positive thinking.

"Listen, Curlytop, I got something to tell you," Jo said.
"Let's take a regular excuse and sit in the gallery."

"I took one last week. I don't need it. They'd know."

"Don't be so chicken. They don't count them. Anyway,
I've got something to tell you about your wonderful K. A.,"
she said, chewing her gum loudly and vulgarly, blowing still
another bubble. She had me and she knew it.

We signed our slips and trotted to the gallery, where we
sat and watched the gym below. It was a basketball day and
the gym resounded with shouting and cheering. Miss Alcott,
in a new navy athletic outfit, moved nimbly over the gym
floor, blowing her whistle when necessary, and stopping from
time to time to demonstrate a correct dribble or the proper
technique for throwing the ball. From this distance I was seeing another Karen Alcott, not the austere remote instructor
but an enthusiastic schoolgirl throwing herself into the game.
The girls on the team responded with a vitality they'd never
shown when Schmidt directed them.

The girls from Dance Club were practicing in the corner
of the gym. They had special dispensation that allowed them
to do this each day. Serious and dedicated, they neither talked
nor smiled but followed an exercise ritual as strictly as
though it were a religious rite. All of them, wearing leotards
and tights, imitated Miss Alcott. Those with short hair encouraged it to grow and those with long hair tied it with a
scarf at the nape of their neck or twisted it into a neat, severe
knot which they pinned to the crown of their head.

Time had not helped. I still ached with the disappointment
of not being part of the group.

"I just can't figure out what you see in her. Like you're in love or something stupid like that," Joanna said.

"In *love*! You're crazy, Jo. I don't know what you're talking about," I answered too strongly.

"I can read what's written all over your face, the way you stare at Alcott all the time with big cow eyes."

"What a dumb thing to say! You're all wrong."

"Cat, you know me. I see right through people. X-ray eyes. I *know* you're tearing yourself apart over old Frigid-bones down there. Did it ever occur to you that she can't stand blacks, Armenians, Puerto Ricans, Jews, and Eye-talians? Like she could be a racist."

"How can you say a thing like that? What proof?"

"Easy. Look at Dance Club. Fifteen girls, twelve of them blue-eyed blondes and the other three obviously WASPS. Didn't you notice?"

"Jo, that's unfair. Anyone could try out. *Anyone*. She couldn't help it if only a few competed. Besides, the girls in the club are good dancers, particularly Linda Holmes. She's studied ballet a long time."

"Okay. But you gotta admit, there are some neat dancers in this school and they're not all blue-eyed blondes. Why do you suppose they didn't even bother to try out?" Joanna made her point, naming three black girls and an outstanding Puerto Rican girl who probably danced better than any girls in the club.

"It just happened that way," I said, determined to defend Miss Alcott. "Anyway, some other black girls did try out but they really weren't that good. I think she was fair, so there."

"I couldn't care less," Joanna said. "I'm just worried about you, Cat, working yourself up over her. Did it ever occur to you she might be gay?"

"Too much, Jo. First you call her a racist. Now she's gay. Let me see you prove that one."

Joanna stared at me, then burst into laughter. "Oh Cat,

you're so serious. You're getting so upset over her. There's no proof at all. Just suspicion. I just think you should stop thinking about her. She's a gym teacher, that's all."

"Is this what you made me take an excuse for?"

"No. I've got real information. If you can tear your eyes away from her for a second, I'll tell you."

Purposely I kept my eyes on the game and on Miss Alcott, who adroitly side-stepped the players in the climax of an exciting game. Then I turned to her.

"All right. What's so special?"

"She comes from an old American family. She told us that. She's probably gone to some fancy schools. Most of the jobs she's had have been in private schools, five of them. What do you suppose she's doing teaching here?"

"She needed a job. Maybe she wanted a different kind of experience."

"Are you kidding? I think she was having a hard time. This is desperation. Or it may have something to do with wanting to be with her roommate."

"What?"

"She lives with a woman, Elizabeth Chapin, who teaches music at Charing School. She's very good-looking, a brunette with brown eyes and short dark hair. She and Alcott live together at Twenty-nine and a half Chauncey Circle. What do you think of that?"

I shrugged my shoulders indifferently, although I could not wait to pick up every crumb I could about Miss Alcott. "How did you find this out?"

"Spies." Jo waited, blew another bubble, then grinned. "It's all in the newspapers for everyone to see. Chapin's students are giving a concert, and all this information was added free. Just thought you'd want to know."

"And to think I wasted a pink slip for this!"

I left feeling ashamed and unfaithful, wondering if what

Joanna said about Miss Alcott's being a racist and a lesbian could be true. Then I put it out of my mind. Miss Alcott was perfect; that was all I had to know about her.

Since the next day in gym was an exercise day rather than a game period, Miss Alcott, a priestess in a lavender leotard and a violet jersey dance skirt, first lectured us on the use and misuse of pink regular slips. "Possibly many of you are not used to discipline. Even punishment for coming in late doesn't matter to you. Let me tell you again: rules are meant to be kept. Without them we would fall apart. I am insistent on obeying rules and following disciplines, because that is the only way anything is accomplished. In the future, anyone dallying with pink slips will be answerable to me. Do you understand?"

As she spoke, her voice took on a metallic quality and her features became unpleasantly sharp. Joanna threw me a glance of triumph, then whispered, mimicking, "We are not used to discipline, not all us ethnic types. See!"

But then Miss Alcott softened, becoming almost conversational again as she told us about the theories of a remarkable dancer named Martha Graham while we sat on the floor, half-dying of perfect posture.

"I once had the privilege of working with this great artist. I spent a year in a concert group that followed her teachings and theories. I learned that when we dance we are doing more than merely using our bodies. Dance is a way of living, of thinking, of breathing. I wish I could give you the essence of what dancing is all about, simply hand it to you, but it's not possible. Each person must find this out for herself, through dedication and practice. At least we can begin to work together here."

She went on to talk of the need for being centered and had us find that place just below our rib cage and above our stomach where our impulses toward movement began. Nobody was quite sure what she was talking about, but she said in time we'd understand and that the exercises we did would release us from our everyday lives and put us in touch with ourselves in a deeper way.

In all our lives, nobody had ever talked to us like that.

"Don't mind if it hurts. Of course it's going to hurt a little."

Groans and mutterings could be heard as soon as we began the routine of exercises, but I was beginning to understand what she meant by the flow as one movement led to another. At rare intervals, a silence fell over the class, as if all of us were sensing what she meant. She walked among us, pointed with a polished stick to that part of someone's back which needed straightening or a fanny that needed to be tucked under. The highest praise she granted was a cool "all right." Now and then she whispered a few words to a girl, either a correction, a suggestion, or possibly praise. I longed to be singled out in some way, but she passed by me without comment.

However, as I was about to leave the gym, she called me.

"D'Amato, come here. I want to see you." Other girls had first names but apparently I would be "d'Amato" forever, never Catherine. Yet she spoke pleasantly enough.

"I want to talk with you. Will you come to my office after school?"

What could she possibly want? All day I worried about the illicit pink slip or that she had overheard my conversation with Joanna or that someone had heard and reported it to her. That would be just my luck!

Then again, maybe someone had dropped Dance Club and she wanted me to take that person's place. I alternated between hope and fear. The day lasted forever until I knocked on the door of her office. After ten minutes, so it seemed, she invited me in.

"You wanted to see me?" My voice dropped to a whisper.

She frowned, then remembered and smiled. "Yes, sit down, Caroline."

"Catherine. My name is Catherine."

"Of course. I hope I'm pronouncing 'd'Amato' right after all this time," she said, smiling. What a change, I was thinking. The light fell on the pale hair and livened the edges of an emerald-scarf tied carelessly over a creamy hand-made sweater. She dressed better than anyone I had ever known.

"Catherine, we need half a dozen posters for the Christmas concert. Dance Club will be doing only one number, 'Green-sleeves,' but even so I'd like publicity. Mr. Everett said you were very good and he'd let you use class time for the project. Do you think you could do it? This is what I had in mind."

She pulled out several stiff, stilted drawings. They were pretty bad, certainly not like anything I would have drawn. But she was *asking* me to do something for her! And Mr. Everett had said I was good! It was almost too much. My face grew red, my throat became dry.

"I think I could do them. But I'd have to see the dances so I could plan the posters."

"No problem. You can come to rehearsals if you like. You'll have to imagine the costumes, but I can tell you about them. In any event, you don't have to be literal about them. All you'll need is one poster. Then you can silkscreen it, if you like. Can I depend on you?"

"Yes, of course!"

"All right then. You can begin on them and let me see them as soon as possible," she said, dismissing me with a nod of her head.

Awkward, jubilant, wanting to shout, I thanked her and left. Something good had happened after all, something far greater than I could have expected. Too happy to walk, I ran all the way to the Mona Lisa.

Chapter Eleven

Now I was a member of the club, in a way of speaking. The afternoon following my interview with Miss Alcott, I slipped shyly into the gym, settled on a bench in the corner, and opened up a new sketchbook. I'd already made arrangements to arrive at the Mona Lisa later each day and I'd also spent more than I should have on new sketchbooks, pencils, inks, and other materials. Off on a drawing binge!

The girls in the club were warming up, some stretching at the bar, two practicing deep pliés, several chatting, while one pulled her hair up into a high knot in imitation of Miss Alcott. Modern Degas studies. Immediately I began to sketch them. Miss Alcott glanced at me once, then turned away and never looked at me again. So I was destined to be invisible here as well as in class!

Just wait until you see my posters, Miss Alcott, I was thinking. You'll never forget me then!

Now I forgave her for not having chosen me to be part of Dance Club. This position, the official artist of the group, suited me more. That, added to my drawings which appeared weekly in the *Gilkie Gazette,* made me wonder, Was I really an artist after all? Could I become one?

As the group rehearsed, my pencil flew. Everything around Miss Alcott, everything concerned with the dancers, was so rich in possibilities, that I nearly filled a sketchbook that first day. Sixteen live models at once! Foolishly I lingered at the end of the rehearsal, expecting that at least some of the girls would want to see what I had drawn, but I could have waited forever. They were so caught up in themselves they didn't know, could not have cared less, that I had been drawing them. Never mind, I comforted my bruised ego, the real excitement lay in watching Karen Alcott. She was emerging from the role of gym teacher to that of the dancer, the artist, the leader of the group.

She was the sun around whom we revolved, and I was not the only one to admire her. Gradually the girls in the club pulled away from other students and associated only with each other, as if they knew a secret they would never share with anyone else. They walked to school together, ate their lunch apart from everyone else, and no longer took part in regular gym classes but practiced by themselves in a far corner. They imitated Miss Alcott's clothes, her walk, her hair, the chiffon scarves she liked to wear, and her cool, dry voice.

And Miss Alcott loved it! She let these girls call her Karen at rehearsals and often became friendly, even confidential, as though they were her associates, yet she never quite gave up the role of priestess. She worked the girls hard, and the more she demanded, the more they responded. Nor did she spare herself. She rehearsed difficult sections of a dance again and again with a concentration such as I'd never seen in anyone, and the girls followed, never complaining. They were caught up in the dance, caught up with Karen herself, and nothing stood in their way. Their lithe bodies slid, circled, arched, and rose while Karen watched or joined them, stopping to correct an awkward spot or shouting, "That's it! That's it!" when a phrase worked out well.

Caught up in the maelstrom of movement, my pencil flew from one drawing to the next and the sketchbooks piled up as I finished them. My style was changing from the black intensity which made Mr. Everett despair to a light, airy shorthand, each movement caught swiftly as it happened. Only a happy artist could have drawn with so light a touch as mine was becoming.

When several drawings of the dancers were printed in the *Gilkie Gazette,* Linda Holmes, the lead dancer, told me they were terrific. "And it's such good publicity for Dance Club, too!"

This was the only comment anyone made except, of course, for the editors of the *Gazette,* who always liked what I did for them. But there was no time for self-pity. Drawing was on me like a fever. I worked some of the quick sketches into frustration. Perspective was difficult. I didn't know enough studied drawings. It was then I could have screamed with about anatomy. Sometimes a brief sketch lost its vitality when expanded to a drawing. And yet it was alive and I was alive doing it.

I had Karen to thank. One word of encouragement and I was living as an artist. Once more, as when I was a child, I wanted to draw forever.

Some of the best sketches came one day during a brief rest when the girls were sitting on the floor. They were clustered around Karen and were making graceful compositions without realizing it. Karen was talking about a professional group she had once belonged to, a New York group that had toured Europe one season. Her eyes became wistful as she confided some of the incidents.

". . . and there we were in Stockholm, two hours before performance, and where were our costumes? Stuck at some airport, probably in Turkey or Athens. What to do? We couldn't dance in our street clothes. Then we were saved by sheer good luck, the most unlikely chance. The man who designed for a Swedish ballet company helped us find leotards and material for the skirts we needed so badly because they were important to some of the dances. So there we were sewing, barely getting the skirts around us when the curtain opened and we had to go on, praying that the new skirts would stay on during the performance!"

More tales of misadventures, such as finding their group scheduled the same night as a group of African dancers; meeting with composers, artists, and dancers, many of whom were so eccentric that she imitated them for us; the terrific beauty of the northern countries and of Paris, with chestnut trees in bloom; and how, at one point, when the company was quite broke, the group took to dancing in night clubs to make enough to keep alive. We hung on her words, the other girls and I, my drawings half-forgotten as I longed for my life to become that exciting.

"But Karen, how could you leave a life like that and come to a dump like Gilkie High?" one of the girls asked. Karen shook her head helplessly.

"I have to make a living," she sighed. "Maybe some of you will become dancers and stay with it longer than I."

There could have been more to the story. How much was there that I would never know about her but only guess? Was Gilkie High only a stopgap for her? Had she given up professional dancing? Maybe she was too old; the thought filled me with sorrow. In any event, she had no wish to talk of it, for she sprang to her feet and the rehearsal went on.

Drawing from live models was becoming a mania for me. I could not stop.

Some of the best models were not the dancers but the girls

in the locker room, for they acted more naturally there, less self-conscious. Half-protected by a curtain, I sat in a dressing stall and sketched the girls as they showered. If anyone glanced at me, I pretended to be scribbling the homework I should have done the night before.

One morning I was caught. Donna Ricci, a large girl whose development had been startling even when she was in the fifth grade, stood in the shower, enjoying the steady downpour of warm water that ran in rivulets down her melon breasts, her heavy belly, and her generous buttocks. I had almost finished a soft pencil drawing that described her in thick, buttery lines yet with the lightness that characterized my new style, when she realized what I was doing.

"Hey you! Who you starin' at? You drawin' me? Gimme that, you bitch. C'mon, gimme," she sputtered in fury as she reached for my sketchbook. She shed water all over it and all over me too, but I hung on to it.

"Quit it, Donna! You're tearing my book. Let me explain!" It was necessary to yell over the sound of the running water and the echoes of the locker room, but she stopped struggling with me. Wrapping a towel around herself, she glared at me and spoke in a voice shaking with anger.

"Who do you think you are?"

"Listen, Donna, I wasn't making fun of you. Honest. You're a terrific model to draw and that's the truth. You can ask any artist. See, I didn't even put in your face."

There was no way of explaining to her that although in her clothes she actually was the pitiful slob she most likely considered herself to be, an embarrassment of bulges, in the nude she bloomed with a certain feminine grace. Later the curves would grow massive and ugly, but at the moment they had a full arabesque quality that I found appealing.

"It's just that I like to draw you. You're a perfect model, Donna. Really."

She hesitated, not knowing whether or not I was making fun of her. She could never know how richly black her drenched hair was against the olive skin, shining in its wetness. Nor could I have told her that Maillol, a great sculptor, would have found her magnificent. She wouldn't know who Maillol was and in any event she wasn't about to trust me.

"You draw me anymore and I'll . . . I'll . . . I'll tear that book of yours into a hundred pieces," she threatened, nearly in tears.

"All right," I said softly, sad because she would never know she was not as ugly as she thought. How helpless I was after all!

After that, I traced the drawings only with my fingers and later sketched what I remembered. One day I would have live models and I could draw without having to rush. More than sketches, large luminous paintings rose before my eyes. I could practically see them, feel the vibrations of the colors and get caught up in the rhythm of the line.

At last I was beginning to dare to believe that I would become an artist. A new daydream evolved. I would live in a studio, a tall, wooden structure with skylights, in some northern country where the light was cool and pure. A place near a lake or the ocean. Possibly the members of Dance Club, now professional, would live nearby, gladly acting as my models. My studio would isolate me only as much as I cared to be alone, but more often than not Karen would come to stay with me, to lunch with me on the simple patio outside, and to pose for me so that I could catch forever her long and lyrical grace.

"How are the posters coming?" Karen asked one day at the end of a rehearsal. She twisted her head to catch a glimpse of a drawing I had just finished, a group pose in brush and sumi ink.

"These are just sketches. I've already blocked out the posters." I dared not call her Karen as the others did.

"May I see your sketches." A royal command, not a question.

"They're just . . . they're not very good," I mumbled as she glanced through the sketchbook. Immediately all the errors of anatomy and proportion and foreshortening loomed as if huge red arrows pointed out each mistake. She flipped through the pages.

"A beginning, isn't it? Would you like to see some pictures of dancers?"

"Yes, thank you. I'd love it."

I followed her into her office. The shelves were lined with books, large expensive coffee-table volumes filled with photographs and drawings (I was sure) of the Russian ballet, ink sketches of Isadora Duncan and large photographs of modern dancers. Briefly she showed me a collection of drawings of Martha Graham, flashing them before me so rapidly I could hardly see them while my own sketchbook fell to the floor and lay there dishonored and pitiful.

"This is really what I want to show you, drawings made by one of my friends," Karen said, pulling out a portfolio nicely bound in red linen. Inside were a dozen watercolors. Seldom have I seen any so forbidding in their coldness, so dead, so utterly without warmth or vitality; and these were supposed to be dancers? Could she really enjoy such stiff, colorless—in spite of the colors, they remained somehow colorless—drawings? I glanced at her as she gazed at them slowly, one at a time. Her lips parted, softened. She even turned to me, "These are so stark, so moving, so without sentimentality and yet so rich, aren't they?" she asked.

I nodded my head dumbly, shocked at her lack of judgment. Then it occurred to me that somebody she loved must have done these colored drawings and it was the artist, not the pictures, that she loved. Immediately I became jealous, not "pangs of jealously" at all, but a feeling that was sharper and more direct, like a knife plunging into me.

"Who did these?" I asked, voice quavering, since it was usually acceptable to ask the name of the artist.

"Frances," she said, then sharply, "I don't think you'd know the artist."

Was it Frances, a woman, or Francis, a man? No matter, I could make a series of drawings even now that would far surpass her work—or his.

I was wishing that Miss Alcott would lend me one of her splendid books, but the thought didn't cross her mind. She replaced the portfolio of drawings and the books and stared pointedly at the clock on the wall.

"I have to get to work. Thanks, Miss Alcott."

"And you will be starting on the posters soon? We want to be sure to have them," she said, in a voice I took to be encouraging. She even smiled a little.

That was my reward. Even before I'd left the office, she was reviewing some papers on her desk, as though I weren't there at all.

"I don't understand why you want to make six separate posters when it's so easy to make one and silkscreen it," Mr. Everett said.

"It's all right. I don't mind," I said. Each poster demanded hours of work, yet I hesitated to finish them until the day before the deadline, for once I handed them in, my excuse to go to rehearsals would be gone.

I worked meticulously in the art room, often doing the

same poster two or three times until it was perfect. One day after school I brought them to Miss Alcott.

"Oh yes, the posters," she said. She shuffled through them quickly while I stood there horrified. She was missing all the nuances of shading, the careful balances, and the colors I had so carefully mixed. The telephone rang, interrupting her brief viewing. Putting her hand over the mouthpiece of the phone, she said, "Thanks. They'll do." and dismissed me with a wave of her hand.

And so it was over. The posters were finished. Elated that I no longer had to worry about them and yet strangely empty without them, I walked out of school into the face of a bitter wind. It was over now, and yet something, I did not know what, remained to be done.

That night my mother and I sat down to an indifferent supper of greasy meatballs and weak coffee. Again I became aware of gloom in the faded walls, the worn-out furniture and the chipped kitchen table where we sat. We said little, since my mother was jelled in a private depression of her own.

After dinner while she collapsed in the womb of her easy chair to comfort herself with another evening of TV, I cleaned up the kitchen and wondered if I were catching cold. I had to keep telling myself Miss Alcott had liked the posters but it was the stiff drawings of Frances Whoever that she admired the most. In another minute I'd be as dejected as my mother.

On the way to my bedroom, I stumbled against a chair and a book of loose sketches dropped to the floor. As I picked them up, I studied them. One was a fairly good drawing of Karen and a sketch of Linda leaping across the floor—there was no mistaking the speed and thrust of the leap. Three figures in the shower, a dozen sketches of Dance

Club drawn as the girls prepared for rehearsal or sat around talking, and best of all sketches of Karen. What would happen to all this work?

They were so much better than Frances's, that I knew. Well then, why not put them in a portfolio. The collection could be called "The Karen Drawings" because they would celebrate her in sketches—Karen dancing, walking sternly among the girls in gym class, shooting a basketball, or holding her hand to her forehead as she tried to answer a difficult question. Of course the other sketches of Dance Club would also be included. And dreams, illusions, fantasies. Suddenly I knew that this was what I'd do next.

I cleaned the kitchen quickly and scrubbed the table carefully before placing my drawings on one side and a pile of drawing paper on the other. Soon I was going through all the sketches, choosing some, rejecting others, planning which ones I would redraw and considering how they should be done.

If the apartment remained glum, I did not notice. The scratches on the walls, the window shade that hung lopsided and would not straighten, the agonized crying of the baby next door . . . they all disappeared. My universe became a circle of lamplight on the kitchen table, a stack of drawings and myself bending over them. Once more I was saved.

Chapter Twelve

A thousand students poured out of school, scattering in the streets, pushing, shouting, singing. Christmas vacation had just begun! A knitted cap was whipped from someone's head and thrown into the air. More caps followed it. A chase began, a fight ensued, a boy and girl stood embracing in the middle of the racket as if nothing were happening, and over all the snowflakes fell, a white benediction, but not enough yet to make snowballs. We were all freezing and noisy and hilarious because of our gift of freedom.

My cousin Tony, violin under his arm, caught up with me to give me a husky hello, a warm grin.

"Hey, Catherine. Long time no see."

"I know. I've missed you. I've been right there in school. And you?"

"Me too. School! What a waste! It takes so much time away from music. I can't wait to get out. What are you doing this vacation?"

"Nothing much. And you?"

"I've got a few jobs, a concert with the orchestra, and

we'll be in New York a few days, having Christmas with my mother's family.

"I meant to tell you, Cat, those posters you did for Dance Club were really first-rate. I liked them. I like your sketches in the *Gazette* better, though."

"You like them? Thanks." Many people had told me they were good and even Mr. Everett was enthusiastic, but Tony's opinion meant more to me than anyone's because Tony knew instinctively what worked and what didn't.

We lingered as the crowds thinned out. I was thinking that if Tony weren't my cousin and if I hadn't known him all my life, I could have fallen in love with him. Possibly it was true for him, too. But as it was, we shared another kind of closeness, almost as if we were brother and sister.

He walked with me to the corner, but just before we crossed the street, the lights changed and we barely escaped being run over by a white sports car that was tearing through the red light. A gift for me! Another glimpse of Karen Alcott, dressed in a white jacket with a white mohair scarf hanging around her neck. She might have seen me out of the corner of her eye . . . one rapid flickering movement there . . . but she gave no sign of recognition. My eyes followed her car until it disappeared.

"Who's that?" Tony asked.

"The gym teacher. Karen Alcott. Don't you think she's beautiful?"

"How would I know! I was too busy trying not to get knocked down. Actually, I had the impression she was kind of a cold fish. Just an impression. Someone like that doesn't appeal to me, not right away. You're prettier."

"Me, prettier? Oh, Tony, what a thing to say! She's superb."

"Is she? Maybe I didn't see that in her. Catherine, I wish

we could go somewhere for coffee. Damn, there's never enough time. I've got to get over to the music school. Maybe we could get together over vacation. Do something. What do you think?"

"Great! Will you call me? I've got to get to work, too. I wish we could go out in the country and walk in the snow . . . oh well. Have a good lesson, Tony. *Ciao!*"

"*Ciao!* I'll be seeing you."

So Tony, like Joanna, didn't like Karen Alcott. And he said I was prettier! I had to laugh at the extravagance of that lie, but it kept me smiling the rest of the day.

All through vacation I prayed for snow, a world of purity, Karen Alcott's world. For me snow is something magic, covering everything with whiteness, as if all life were going to begin again. Maybe that's one of the reasons I kept seeing Karen as coming from the far north, a place where she could skate on frozen rivers and ski down mountain slopes. She had told the gym classes she would be attending a dance conference in Montreal and I imagined her there, dashing down white city streets while the snowflakes flurried around her as if she were a figure in one of those glass balls which snowed when it was shaken.

But *our* snow, like the flurry that hailed the beginning of winter vacation and died before it was half an hour old, was slow in coming. A chilling wind blew newspapers and rubbish along the street and sidewalks. On Lily Street an occasional brave Christmas tree glowed in a window as the year drew toward its desolate end. People suffered the lowering temperatures with bent shoulders and slow, shuffling steps. Even the children who played in the streets shivered in the wind and succumbed to the gloom.

The only person who could revel in such a cold world

was one born to it, a Karen Alcott, a snow queen. On my bedroom wall I had tacked some drawings; one, a portrait in charcoal and pastel on gray paper, showed the structure of fine bones in a long porcelain face, the delicate hollows and the slightly sharp nose. When I half-closed my eyes and shifted the features, I saw there a bird, a cool northern bird that defied wind and snow.

"Catherine, you're a gem!" Mrs. Russo beamed. She touched the top of my head with her well-manicured fingers and sighed. "What I'd like to give you for Christmas is a good haircut, but if you're not ready for it, I'll have to wait." She sighed again. I think that hair in its natural state upset her, particularly when it was as wildly natural as mine. "You've been real good, so here's a Christmas bonus. Enjoy!"

I hugged her, careful not to upset her coiffure of heavily sprayed curls. My mother remarked sourly that Mrs. Russo liked me because she could get me for less than minimum wage, which was true, but in her way, she may really have liked me and fretted over me, too, almost as if I were a daughter. The bonus, a gift which she didn't have to give me, pleased me no end, as did Mrs. Russo's indulgent smile. "Spend it on yourself now."

I had already bought my mother her present, an extravagance of cosmetics—vials of eye creams, lipstick and eye shadow, hormone moisturizers and small bottles of perfume, all handsomely packaged in a box covered with French-blue material. (Oh yes, she would love it!) So I immediately went downtown to spend my bonus on a gift for myself. Searching through several stores, I finally found the soft off-white sweater I craved, a poor imitation of Miss Alcott's hand-knit mohair shirt-sweater, but close. I also found a bone half-wool, half-nylon skirt that could have been a poor relation of her tailored outfit.

"Not bad," I thought, approving of all three Catherines in the three-way mirror of the store.

"White in winter, Catherine? It won't work," my practical mother said when she saw it that evening. "You'll have to clean it every time you wear it. Believe me, you'll be sorry. Take it back. Do you still have the receipt?"

"But I like it," I said grudgingly. My mother wasn't being angry, only motherly. What kind of person thinks first of grime and cleaning bills and labels that say DRY CLEAN ONLY when it's such a luxury to wear something light?

"Listen, darling. When they advertise winter white, it's for clothes that can be washed or for rich people who can afford to take stuff to the cleaners each time they wear it. Be sensible. Go downtown tomorrow and exchange it."

"No," I said, pursing my lips, refusing to argue.

"Why are you so *difficult?*" she exploded at last, but I didn't answer or apologize, nor did I intend to exchange my precious sweater and skirt for something more reasonable.

Vacation dragged. Though I worked at the Mona Lisa longer hours and baby-sat twice for Aunt Mary, I thought of nothing but Karen Alcott. Where was she, when would I see her again, would she ever like me? Again and again the same questions came up until I couldn't stand them anymore.

I invented fantasies. In a dream she begged me to do her portrait, something wanted for a national exhibition, and she invited me to move in with her and Miss Chapin to finish this oil portrait, a full-length, life-size pose in luminous pinks with touches of pale color.

During the day I embroidered variations on this theme. In my mind weekends were spent driving up to Vermont in the Triumph to go skiing. Once we took a spontaneous trip to the beach for a winter picnic. On another occasion there was a weekend flight to California and a Sunday afternoon spent in front of the fireplace, drinking hot chocolate and telling stories. All these imaginary events added up to a towering fantasy. And more . . . bit by bit Karen would confide in me, giving me the story of her life and her innermost thoughts. One day she would tell me how much she needed me. She would put her arm around me. . . .

This was the picture I held in my mind the night my mother went to a Christmas party. I was spreading out the poisonous blue powder that was meant to discourage a fresh invasion of cockroaches in the kitchen, when I bumped into the truth as though it were a wall.

"Idiot!" I yelled out loud, scolding myself. Who was I fooling with all this nonsense about Karen Alcott, who had never smiled at me, who would hardly acknowledge my existence, who could not remember my name? This was my life, this cockroach-infested kitchen, the hair that had to be swept from the Mona Lisa floor each day, and the school that made no sense. This endless daydreaming, these fantasies, which filled the meaningless hours of the days, why, they were drugs, like grass or coke.

I knew I had to drop the habit. Forget her. Begin somewhere else, but where? Well, there was Rita Blomberg. I liked her and every time I gave her a drawing for the *Gazette,* she said we must get together sometime. I dialed her number, hopeful now that we could meet somewhere for a cup of coffee and a good long talk. Her phone rang five times and then I gave up.

Then I would draw, another kind of release. I took out a new sketchbook, settled down to a still life, either the plants in the window or whatever pots and pans happened to be on the stove, a subject not as easy as it might first appear. Life as it was. I spent an hour drawing a geranium, a detail of my mother's prized Boston fern, and a composition of pans.

So what! Before long other images appeared, a long line here, a certain curve there and they all turned into sketches of dancers resembling Miss Alcott.

A hopeless case.

Chapter Thirteen

C hristmas Day always meant dinner at Aunt Carol's
and Uncle Frank's.

"Mom, do we have to go this year?"

"Of course. What else would we do? Where else would
we go?"

"It's so boring. It will be like every other Christmas, except we'll all be a year older."

"Don't complain. Count your blessings."

It wouldn't be so bad, I thought, if Anthony and Joanna
were there, but Anthony's mother, my aunt Flora, "a foreigner from New York," always hovered at the edge of the
family and was never quite admitted to the sisterhood of my
mother, Aunt Carol, and Aunt Mary. As for Joanna and her
mother, Aunt Carol always remarked what a pity it was there
wasn't enough room for them.

But my grandparents and great-grandmother, who was my
grandfather's mother, would be there and that would make
it worthwhile. Each December they drove in to spend the
Christmas holiday with as many of their nine children and as
many of their grandchildren as would be there. Each time I
saw them it came to me that I really loved them in a way

I couldn't ever love anyone else, and yet they moved slowly, their English was broken, they said little, as though they were not part of the same world my aunts and uncles inhabited. But when I looked into their old eyes, I could tell that nothing escaped them.

In November my mother had made an enormous, rich fruitcake to which she kept adding rum, certain that everyone would praise her so lavishly for it that she could forget to be jealous of her sister's handsome house in a new, fashionable suburb. We could expect an hour of hugging and kissing, exaggerated compliments for someone's dress or someone's child or someone's promotion to a better job and then voices would lower, heads would shake, and tongues would *tsk-tsk* as the harder family news would be discussed in secret whisperings which I, not yet an adult, was not supposed to hear. Then we would sit at the dinner table with its ivory damask cloth, the silver bowl filled with roses, and the candles burning in gold candelabra. Aunt Carol always puts on a great show—place cards, fish forks, and all.

But it would be my grandparents who would sit at the head of the table. My grandfather—Nonno—would look around slowly at everyone there and for once everyone would become silent and even bow their heads out of respect; then he would give his blessing, and make a short speech, first in Italian, followed by an English translation nobody could ever make head or tail of, and then we would all drink wine and wish each other good health and happiness. That was the part I liked the best. I felt so proud to have such a dignified grandfather. And my grandmother—Nonna—who sat beside him, was always staunch, erect, and kind. But I think she wished they were having Christmas in her house, as they used to do, and that made her a little sad.

"There's nothing like a family!" my mother chirped for at least a week before Christmas. Family, family, family! She talked of it until I wanted to yell at her to shut up. At every family festival she fought with herself, two sides of a coin. At first she would be loud and boisterously pleased at being with everyone again. Then she would drink too much wine and sing too loudly. Before the evening was over, she would have had words with her brother Sal, for which I cannot blame her because he teases. Worse than that would be the pain in her eyes as she praised the extravagant gifts Uncle Frank had given Carol, either diamond jewelry, a new stereo, or a fur coat. Oh my poor mother!

So I didn't really look forward to Christmas dinner.

It happened exactly as I expected. While Aunt Mary sat nursing the baby and her other children ran around, grabbing the imported chocolates which Aunt Carol had unwisely set out in silver dishes, I was wishing I were one of them, six years old again, wild and allowed to get away with it because it was Christmas. At this point, I was no longer a child and not yet an adult, so I wanted to go home. It was an uncomfortable situation. The festivities had just begun and already I was asked three times when I was going to grow a few inches and when I was going to cut my hair.

If only Joanna were there . . .

"Catherine, come look at Gloria's drawings!" my mother yelled at me across the broad expanse of the living room. Without even pretending to be modest, Aunt Carol had taken Gloria's work from her room to show it off. Now everyone was competing to see who could praise her most.

"Remarkable!"

"What a talent!"

"And she's so pretty, too. That girl, God love her, has everything."

"Catherine," my mother said loudly enough so that everyone could hear, "see what can be done if only you try. Gloria's sold three of these fashion drawings for fifty dollars each. If you'd just stop doing those dark things . . ."

I remained silent. Gloria's fashion drawings—neat, stiff, and empty—were exactly the sterile sort of pictures Karen Alcott would love. I found myself going tense with jealousy. I wanted to kick my mother. My drawings were better; I *knew* they were better, but who would ever know. Was I fooling myself then?

Gloria, embarrassed, apologized for her mother. "I'm sorry, Catherine. I wish my mother wouldn't make so much of it. It's so humiliating. And you're a real artist. Aunt Mary was telling me . . ."

"That's okay, Gloria. I understand. That's the family," I said, interrupting her so she wouldn't think she had to make me feel better. I wasn't really jealous of her after all, because she was very kind, always had been. Besides, my drawings were better than hers, even if nobody knew except Aunt Mary, who now was trying to get in a word.

"But you should see the portraits that Catherine did of the children! They are gorgeous and they look just like the kids. I had them all framed. It cost plenty but George and I wouldn't have it any other way. The colors . . ."

Sweet Aunt Mary tried too hard to make me a rival when I didn't want to be one, but all conversation stopped when Josie came up to announce that Bianca had just wet her pants. Aunt Carol turned pale. Was it on the new rug, that two-thousand-dollar rug that Uncle Frank had bought her for Christmas, that this happened? The art discussion was over.

When at last we all sat down for dinner and my grand-father got up to give the blessing, his gaze resting for a moment on each one at the table, then in that moment, though we all led separate lives, we were all together again, mysteriously joined.

We all ate too much good food and drank too much wine. At last, in this impressive house and bountiful table which quieted the family, tongues began to loosen. My uncle Sal began to sing and my mother, who had a loud, vigorous voice herself, encouraged everyone else to sing, too.

What would Karen Alcott have thought of it, I wondered. Would she have found us loud, noisy, vulgar?

After dinner as we sat in the living room sipping espresso in small gold cups and the men lit their cigars, filling the room with smoke, the younger children were asked to perform, a family tradition. Dolly played a stumbling minuet on the grand piano. Joey imitated all the TV performers he knew from Big Bird to Baretta and would have gone on all night if Uncle Frank hadn't told him tactfully that we'd have to throw away our TV sets and hire him if he kept on. Bianca stood up and sang ten endless verses of a song she had learned, something about a sparrow and an angel. One small tot, Frankie, scratched on a half-size violin in a pitiful imitation of the now famous Anthony. Each child was applauded, no matter how the performance went, picked up, kissed, praised, and encouraged. Gloria winked at me, which seemed to say, "Remember when we had to perform?" and "Thank God we're free from the painful show and tell." But it had been wonderful to be praised, kissed by hopeful aunts and uncles, and told what a precious thing you were.

And we *still* had to perform but in more subtle ways.

"Do you have a boyfriend yet?" Uncle Frank asked me later that evening.

"You asked me that last year, Uncle Frank, and the year before that."

"It's never too early. I guess you know Theresa will be announcing her engagement one of these days. And Sue's got this crazy idea she wants to go to college first and then become a lawyer. It's ridiculous. I guess you're too sensible to think of things like that."

"I don't know," I mumbled. He couldn't wait to get all of us married off—daughters, nieces, even my mother.

"Of course Gloria's got so many young men eating out of her hand, I don't know how she does it. Maybe she can lend you a few boyfriends."

"No, thank you," I said so sharply that Uncle Frank took the cigar out of his mouth and stared at me. First it was Gloria's clothes and now it was her leftover boyfriends I was supposed to accept gratefully.

"You're a cute kid," Uncle Frank said and left. Five minutes later Uncle Sal came over for a chat—the usual things, how was I, how was Mother, where was my brother, and at last the unavoidable question. "Where's the boyfriend, Catherine? You got one yet?"

I was about to leave before he told me I wasn't getting any younger and should think about getting married. However, the doorbell rang and Gloria's "young man" appeared. The party stopped in rude silence to stare at this handsome Italian prince, whom Uncle Frank proudly introduced as a junior at Yale. Gloria, who had changed to an evening dress, swept into the room sporting a new fur coat, kissed everyone good night sweetly, and apologized for leaving but it was a long way to the dance and it was for a good cause and she'd been on the committee and *had* to go though she hated to leave us. And so on. Her young man—as they all referred to him—shook hands with the men and bowed his head respectfully to all the women. Then he took Gloria's arm and they left.

It was all like a play, as if everyone in the family were given roles to play, for they invariably acted exactly as expected. Gloria would always be glorious in every way; Aunt Carol, ambitious and showy; Aunt Mary, mothering and religious; and my mother, the unlucky one, wandering between poles of ecstasy and misery.

And what was my role? Who was I? Where did I belong? Truth poured out of my wine-filled head. Nowhere. No boyfriend, no art sales, no beauty, no brains (like Sue), no nothing to show for sixteen years of existence. And if I weren't there, I wouldn't be missed. No loss. My mother would find herself a husband. Memory of me would sink like a stone thrown in a lake.

"Mom, I got a headache. Please, can we go home now?"

"Just a minute, just a *minute*. Don't rush me."

Half an hour later Uncle Sal drove us home. Dreams of Karen Alcott cleared away the smoke, the noise of voices, the heavy wine. Once more fantasies curled in my head, comforting me, saving me from those gloomier thoughts I dared not keep. I breathed her name over and over again into my lonely pillow and at last fell asleep.

On December thirty-first I worked at the Mona Lisa until after seven-thirty, for Mrs. Russo was rushed with customers wanting to "get done" before the big New Year's parties. I walked home alone, catching on my tongue the small, slow flakes of snow that were drifting through the air.

My mother, half-dressed for a party that would be given by two "girls" in the office where she worked, apologized, wanting to go and yet guilty about leaving me alone on New Year's Eve. Why couldn't I have the kind of friends who gave parties? she wanted to know.

"I don't mind being alone, Mom. Go and have a good time. It's okay."

"Catherine, you know I love parties. Sometimes you can be very understanding. Sweet."

"You too, Mom."

Neither of us was particularly considerate or sweet and we knew it well. Still, when my mother was good, she was very, very good. That night she set the table with a small embroidered cloth from Italy and what was left of the "best" dishes, pieced together with melamine plates, and a candle in a Chianti bottle. She had bought a round plastic container of *antipasto*—a mosaic of olives, anchovies, peppers, capers, and pickled tomatoes—a green salad with garlic and olive oil, a freshly baked bread, sweet butter and rich coffee, a strong Italian roast. Someday I would paint a still life of that good supper.

"Mom, this is my favorite meal of all meals. No kidding. Better than what we had at Aunt Carol's."

"Come on, now! That was a feast. Those oysters, the roast duck, those cheeses. . . . This is just . . . just . . . " She never knew how to take a compliment with a pleased thank-you, but I could tell she was happy.

"Anyway, I'm not so crazy about Aunt Carol's house. You can practically see the price tag on everything, and I like you better than her."

I thought I'd get my mother drunk on compliments, but immediately she had to defend Carol, who was a loyal Italian daughter, a good wife, a perfect mother ("Just see how good her daughters are turning out!"), yet someone who worked hard for the church and had a heart as big as outdoors. Didn't she give me all of Gloria's old clothes every year?

"Yeah, yeah. But I still like you better."

My mother pinched my cheek affectionately, leaned over, and kissed me. What I said was not untrue, but I wasn't as sweet as I seemed, because I really welcomed the chance of staying home alone.

After she left, I gave myself an exhibition of drawings, setting out pictures all over the sofa, the tables, the chairs, and even the TV. Hundreds of drawings, a room full of drawings. If some were better than I expected, too many were not good enough. Outside on Lily Street, children were exulting in the snow that was at last coming down in thick, moist flakes. They were already banging lids of garbage cans together to make noise while they shouted "Happy New Year" over and over again. It was making me feel old and alone.

The doorbell rang. "Be careful who you let in," my mother had warned before she left. She was a great one for imagining catastrophes and I'd scare myself to death if I listened to her. Yet I paused.

"Hey, Cat, aren't you going to let me in?"

"Joanna!" I flung open the door. We hugged each other and danced around foolishly.

"I gotta go to a party, but it won't begin until eleven or so. So here I am! What's all this stuff you've got around the room, Cat?"

Before I could answer, the doorbell rang again. This time it was Anthony, without his violin. Happy New Year again! We embraced and kissed quickly, but when he saw Joanna, he grew more reserved.

"Let's have some wine!" I cried, all sparkling now, so happy I didn't need anything to drink, but I took out a bottle anyway and three glasses. We drank, holding the glasses high. "To next year!"

I filled Joanna's glass again while Tony picked up a few drawings and examined them.

"Catherine, this is good."

"No, Tony, please, it's just stuff. Let me put it away," I insisted, beginning to gather up the sketches, but Tony said he had to see them all.

"Isn't she great?" Joanna kept saying until I filled her glass for the third time and that shut her up.

"Yeah. Some of these are terrific," Tony said. "I like these life studies."

He held up five sketches, all of them of the girls in the

club, and then he picked up a portrait of Karen, frowned at it, and was about to say something, but apparently thought better of it. It bothered me that he didn't like it. He picked up another one, a fantasy drawing of Karen flying through a snowy sky and this time he shook his head, as if it were awful.

"Come on, that's enough of that!" I cried, gathering up the drawings and putting them away while he and Joanna nibbled at the cookies my mother left. Why didn't he like the drawings of Karen, when he thought the others were good? Still, this was no time to talk of it.

"It's hot in here and it's wonderful out," Tony said. "Let's go and make snowballs."

"I know! Let's go to the park!" Joanna said.

I put on my jacket and draped a muffler around my neck. We went out, made a few snowballs to throw at telephone poles, and then, half-racing and half-walking, made our way to the avenue, took a bus, and rode to Victoria Park.

It was a holiday and the evening was ours. We were becoming children again, chasing each other with mittens full of snow, gathering up handfuls to swallow and throwing snowballs. We made "angel wings" by lying down and moving our arms up and down in the cold, white snow. A small boy let us try his new sled when we asked him and promised him we'd come right back, and so, shouting, we slid to the bottom of the hill, where we overturned and fell into the snow. We brushed each other off and climbed to the top again. Was it because we were a little drunk that we laughed so much or was it this impulsive holiday that made everything so hilarious? When we gave the boy his sled, he shook his head, "Wow, you guys are silly."

"We sure are, honey," Joanna said, giving him a kiss on the tip of his nose.

The sky was a sapphire blue so deep it was nearly black, but it was hard to see because the pure, moist flakes of snow were still coming down to cover everything.

"Damn, wouldn't you know that just when I'm having a good time, I gotta go home and get dressed for a party!" Joanna said.

"You'll have fun."

"This was more fun, being with you guys. Anyway, Happy New Year! G'night, Cat! And Tony, you handsome old thing!"

She hugged me and then planted a long sensuous kiss on Tony, who became embarrassed, pleased, and sheepish all at once. She skipped away and actually hailed a taxi, a sign of impossibly good luck. Tony laughed as if it were all a joke.

The tempo of the evening changed once Joanna left. We walked slowly through the park under a grove of towering evergreens. Occasionally a branch tipped and showered us with fresh snow and we had to stop to brush each other off.

"Cat, you're terrific."

"Me? I'm nothing. It's you, Tony. You've got everything waiting for you. In all this family you're the only one . . ."

"Not the only one. But I hope I'll be good, that I'll get somewhere. Don't put yourself down, Catherine. You can draw, really."

"I don't know. I can't tell. When you were looking at my drawings before . . ."

"They were good."

"But you didn't like all of them. They bothered you. I could tell. Those were the ones I liked most. What was wrong with them?"

"The ones of that woman. I don't know. They just didn't come off for me. I don't know so much about drawings, but they weren't quite there. . . . The drawings of the girls were genuine; I could really believe them. The others . . . well . . . so what do I know about it?"

"I trust your judgment. You thought the ones of the

woman were hokey, is that what you meant? I don't see it that way. That's what bothers me sometimes, that what appears right to me is terrible in someone else's opinion and vice versa. Am I weird? Is there something wrong with me? Am I kidding myself? My mother thinks I should forget all about it. What if she's right?"

"It's not easy when you feel you're all alone. I lucked out. My mother gave me her father's violin when I was three and that's all there was to it. I had a good teacher; he sent me on to a better one; there were scholarships. But even so I've got plenty to learn. Even with luck—my parents, my teachers and all that—it still takes lots of work and more than that, real guts. You have to find out who *you* are."

"And you know, Tony. It's a beautiful thing. Like Nonna would say, the angels kissed you. Sometimes when a drawing comes out well, I think maybe if they didn't exactly kiss me, they patted me on the head. Other times I'm not so sure. I lose my confidence."

"You're not the only one, Cat. You just have to stay with it."

"Tony, do you think that we're different from the rest of the family? Sometimes I wonder what I'm doing here. I almost come to the point of making believe I was mixed up with some other baby in the hospital. Of course I know it's not true."

"We're only a *little* different. What we are may not be like our fathers and mothers but those genes come from our grandparents, and our great-grandparents, and way back. What's the matter, is the family getting to you? Too many Christmas dinners at Carol's?"

I laughed. "How did you know? The trouble is that it's all so mixed up. There's a lot of loving there. I love Nonna and Nonno the most; what wonderful grandparents. They're so dignified. I only wish they weren't so stubborn about my mother and the divorce. And I love Aunt Mary and the kids and almost everyone else. It's not a matter of liking or not liking. It's just that sometimes I feel like I'm in a box and they're sitting on the lid and it's closing down on me. Why don't I get a haircut, why don't I have a boyfriend, why don't I draw like Gloria."

"But all that's so petty. It shouldn't matter."

"It's more than that. Did you ever notice that all the family ever talks about is the family, as if there weren't a world outside?"

"Maybe we're lucky after all. When everybody moved from Ravenna Street and Commercial Street, we were just outside the limits. So we're still in the old place. My folks are still old country in many ways, not at all modern like Carol or your mother. But I know what you mean. It can be oppressive."

We walked slowly through the park, paused beside the pond and watched the snow come down. "It's so pure. I love snow. I don't want to talk about trouble anymore. Let's just watch the snow."

"What I love is the quiet," he said after a while. "It's almost like a sound. Everyone's making noise at parties everywhere, but this silence says more."

"I could stay here forever, Tony, but are you beginning to freeze?"

"I thought you'd never ask!" We walked out of the park and down the snowy streets, past the dark houses and those bright houses that were sparkling with parties. Horns blared, whistles blew, an amplified band drowned the world in rock, then died suddenly. A car shot past us and someone yelled "Happy New Year."

At Sambo's we stopped for hot chocolate, sat across from each other in a booth, and talked. Mostly it was Tony who spoke—about music school, the teachers who believed in him so, the concert, and Juilliard where he would go, with luck. At any rate, he'd be going to New York that summer to study.

"You should go there too, Cat. Museums, galleries, good art schools."

He was trying to encourage me, widen my vision, and give me new hope. I'd never felt so close to anyone and so grateful. He walked me home and left me at the door. We wished each other "Happy New Year" solemnly, not as an overused phrase but a carefully thought sentiment. A thought flickered through my mind, that if I had a boyfriend, it would solve everything; then the thought disappeared. I watched Tony's sturdy, dark figure as he walked down the snowy street. Then I went into the house.

Chapter Fourteen

She was back, she was back! More than once I had awakened from nightmares in which Karen Alcott lay in the snow grotesquely twisted, killed in a skiing accident. Another time I dreamed of her drowning, a dream so vivid that from it I painted a watercolor of Karen drifting, the pale hair spread out in the green waters while sea plants curved in the waves and fish swam by in jewelled colors.

None of it happened! On Monday morning she stood before us in a new white leotard, white tights, and a honeyed skin. She explained she had gone to New Mexico to get some sun, leaving Canada far behind. Smiling broadly, her eyes were brilliant with new hope and resolutions for all of us, but the class gathered slowly, lazy after the holidays.

"Good morning, everyone! Well, it's a new year and it's time to make a resolution. One good resolution is all you need, to become new women. Proud women. Everyone now, stand straight and tall wherever you are. First, I want to look at you."

Possibly a third of the class sprang to attention, but the others slumped, some of them more than they would ordinarily, hostile at her intense enthusiasm and determined smile. I suspected she had decided to win everyone over and transform all of us into "her girls." She walked among us, regarding each girl in turn, tapping a rounded shoulder or a bulging tummy, and waiting until the posture was corrected before moving on. Often though, the minute she passed, the corrected girl would collapse into a slump. Poor Karen! She was trying. I waited for her, standing so erect she would *have* to find me perfect.

"If you hold your breath anymore, d'Amato," she said, "you'll fall over. You have my permission to breathe."

The girls around me tittered. I tried to find kind humor in the comment but the coldness of her voice was all I heard.

"All right," she said when she had checked everyone. "We have a long road ahead of us. You can all use some trans-formation. Too many things here won't pass—sloppy pos-ture, uncombed hair, and odors. Yes, some of you might bathe more often. I also wonder what you've been stuffing yourself with this vacation—pizza? Spaghetti? Junk food? Tomorrow we'll have weigh-ins and talk diet."

At the words *pizza* and *spaghetti,* Joanna shot a look my way, as if to say, "See, I was right. She has it in for us."

"Now don't be discouraged. Today I want to show you that it's possible to change," Miss Alcott continued, not unkindly but with the expression that suggested she was going to convert us and we were going to love it, whether we liked it or not. "Please sit down."

We plunked ourselves on the cold and not-too-clean gym floor. She half-shut her eyes, as if our awkwardness hurt her.

"Get up and try again. Move like women, not rhinoc-eroses."

She herself floated to a sitting position with such ease that we despaired of ever doing so well. Comments were muffled but audible. "Goddamn finishing school" was among them.

"There, that was better. Today we'll talk about beauty. Do you ever think of it? Of course you do. Some of you may think it's a matter of having a certain skin color or the shape of your features or the figure you inherited, as if it were a matter of luck, but that's not necessarily the case. Do you know why? I'll tell you. Beauty lies within you. Each of you can be as beautiful as you want to be. It's the *spirit* within you that makes it possible. Here is the center from which it flows."

She put her hand on her diaphragm, the long fingers touching her ribs as she stretched her long catlike back. Some tried to imitate her.

"First let us breathe in, hold the breath for six counts, and then let it out slowly."

Were we to have half an hour of breathing then? That was dull. Happily for us, after the first two breaths she continued with her lecture, speaking so earnestly I wondered if she really cared about us or if she was trying to win us over for some other reason, to gratify her own ego or whatever.

"Beauty begins here. The first step is to hold ourselves proud and straight. Have you ever noticed that when a dog stands at attention, the ears are pricked upward, the spine is stretched and you can sense his alertness. It is that alertness we must try to achieve. Then we will move beautifully.

"When you *want* to be beautiful, you change your life. It comes with *wanting*. You'll eat only those foods that will do good things for you and not turn to fat. You'll want to keep yourselves meticulously clean. Think beauty! Your lives will become harmonious. You'll wear the clothes that are right for *you*. You'll make your environments harmonious."

A buzz of comment, not all of it complimentary, followed the lecture.

"Hey, Miz Alcott," one girl spoke out. "If we ain't got money for creams and oils and harmonious environments and all that, and if our mothers feed us pizza and tacos, what are we supposed to do about it?"

"I'm glad you asked that," Miss Alcott said tactfully, although I was sure she wasn't entirely happy about it. "It's not going to be easy for several reasons. Lack of money is one, although you won't need as much as you may think. Not having freedom to choose your meals may be another. It's not always easy to tell your mother you want green salad, not macaroni. Someone in your family may laugh at you or try to put you down. But *you can overcome these obstacles.*

"How? Before you change in outward ways, you must develop a strong unshakable desire to make something of yourself. This desire is a seed that grows within you. Once it's there, you'll find ways of becoming beautiful. Your imagination will begin to work; you will become creative; you will make it happen. The will to do it is more important than money. I know this is true."

A small murmur of disbelief buzzed here and there, but she was winning converts. Most of us wanted to believe what she was saying.

"You think I don't understand your problems? I'm going to show you slides of girls and women who began life under harsh circumstances and who became magnificent in spite of it. But first I want to mention something you can begin to do right now and it won't cost you a cent or cause an argument. You can improve your posture. That's the first thing. Then there's the matter of obesity, being fat. Remember, *you can never be too thin.* I, for one, never eat foods that I like. Every time you eat something, ask yourself, what is this going to do *for* me or *to* me."

Groans followed, weaker now than before. She was winning us over. But why? Even Joanna was listening to her, but her eyes became green slits, waiting for the joker, if there was one, to appear.

"What does it mean to walk straight and hold yourself erect? It means you respect yourself; you are not groveling in self-pity . . . and I must say I see a lot of that around here. We begin by directing our lives, not being pushed."

"I don't think so, Miss Alcott," someone disagreed, a snip of a sophomore named Mary Thorne, who loved to argue. "It's too simple to say you can direct your life, make yourself beautiful and all that. It's luck. It's fate. And you don't have anything to say about it." Someone applauded.

"That's what I call a defeatist's way of regarding life," Miss Alcott answered, eyes flashing. She always pretended to encourage discussion, but it seemed to make her angry when anyone disagreed with her. "It's a matter of will power. I can prove it to you. Let's look at the slides I've been collecting and you'll understand how other people overcame what you would call their fate. A picture's worth a thousand words."

We moved to the corner of the gym where the screen and projector were already set up. Some of us walked with determined alertness and self-conscious good posture while others lumbered with exaggerated clumsiness, as if to spite Miss Alcott.

"First we'll see a series of pictures of girls and women— all kinds, all ages—as well as slides of dancers. These will speak for themselves. One thing they'll prove is that beauty is more than make-up plastered over your face and a closetful of clothes. Let's begin then."

We saw a series of what must have been more than a hundred slides, showing children, girls, young women, and very old women. She didn't say much; she didn't have to. The slides, one coming rapidly after another, made their point. Among them I remember in particular:

> A repulsively fat woman sitting on the subway, legs apart and the heavy thigh flesh spilling over.
>
> Three slender girls running across a green lawn. ("Where we gonna get a lawn like that, Miz Alcott?" someone asked.)
>
> A slender model from the atelier of Yves St. Laurent. (Miss Alcott had to explain that St. Laurent was a designer and an *atelier* was a studio.)
>
> A strong straightforward girl, athletic, an Olympic swimmer. ("She's fifteen years old, girls.")
>
> A queenly bare-breasted African dancer.
>
> Katharine Hepburn standing on her head. ("She's over sixty, girls," Miss Alcott said.)
>
> A serious young girl, not pretty, with glasses, rounded shoulders and an armful of books. Possibly Italian or Jewish. (Everyone laughed and suddenly I hated them all because I could see the sensitivity in this girl's face and knew she was probably very nice and that life wasn't easy for her. For a second I almost hated Miss Alcott, for she meant to have us scorn this girl.)

"And now I have a series of dancers to show you," she said. "Many kinds of dancers. It's taken me a long time to make this collection."

The slides were remarkable, all in color, and as they flashed on the screen, one after the other, I forgot I was angry with Miss Alcott. Among the slides:

> Martha Graham's proud sculptural head.
>
> Girls leaping across an outdoor stage somewhere in California.

A row of French cancan dancers kicking high.

Ballet girls at rehearsal (a long series of these).

Small girls in leotards practicing pliés.

Young Indonesian dancers with elaborate headdresses.

A modern dancer of unquestionable dignity, followed by another slide, a close-up portrait. ("When you examine the features of this dancer, you can see they're not very beautiful. Her nose is too long and bulbous, her chin recedes, and her figure is not that good. But when you meet her, when you watch her dance, you are never aware of her shortcomings . . . including short legs . . . because this dancer has what I want you to have, *a sense of beauty.*")

The hope was beginning to rise in me. Could I change too? I so wanted to become more beautiful! Then a slide came which actually stopped my breath. The girl on the screen, could that have been me, could that have been a sister of mine?

"She looks like Catherine!" someone shouted and a few girls agreed. So it was not just in my imagination after all.

"The girl in this slide," Miss Alcott explained, "the one with the short, curly hair, is a dancer in a New York group. When she began to study, she had no parents, no money, no place to go. As you can see, she's very short and, frankly, she wasn't even a good dancer, but she had the will to work. Belief in herself. She's worked very hard and is making a name for herself. Now there's someone to admire."

"Looks exactly like Catherine," someone said again, but Miss Alcott paid no attention to the remark.

If she could become beautiful, then maybe I could, too, I thought. The resemblance was uncanny, the dark halo of curly hair, eyes that were too large, and a nose that turned up like mine. Yet she was marvelous to look at and I wasn't. It was that studious girl with the books that I was like, not that I resembled her, but I understood her as though she were myself. This one had a kind of nerve about her. So perhaps if I didn't let myself get pushed into desperation, if I didn't get beaten down by my own self-pity, maybe I could become admirable, like the girl in the slide.

Now the new year was beginning for me. Now. *A new year*. If Miss Alcott could applaud a girl who looked like me, then maybe if I were to change, to grow, to become an artist, she would admire me too, maybe she could even like me. That was what I wanted more than anything in the world. I would *earn* her admiration then, starting that very day.

That afternoon I worked so vigorously at the Mona Lisa that even Mrs. Russo noticed. "Starting the new year right, are you?"

The women in front of the mirrors did not know it was a new year, for they never changed but sat, now as before, complaining of the government, taxes, schools, children, husbands, bad health, and thinning hair. Wearing identical plastic aprons, they stared wearily at their reflections in the mirror as their hair was snipped, combed out, and coaxed into curlers.

Never would I be one of them. Never.

At six, when my work was finished, I asked Mrs. Russo if I could borrow an apron and some scissors.

"Catherine, don't tell me you want to cut your hair."

"If you don't mind."

"What's got into you? Look, darling, if you can wait a few minutes, I'll do it for you. I know just how it should be— parted, pulled to the side, maybe a little straightening."

"Thanks, but I'd rather do it myself. I know just how I want it."

The close-cropped coiffure of the small, dark dancer was what I must have; the mass of wild curls was a mistake, too top-heavy for the rest of me.

I wrapped the plastic apron over my clothes and sat in the chair farthest away from where the hairdressers were working. I brushed my hair vigorously and then began to cut the heavy load which fell to the floor in large, long clumps. The hairdressers winked at each other and even the customers cracked their faces enough to smile in a superior way. Let them laugh then, the hags! I concentrated on the reflection in the mirror. My head felt pounds lighter as a bushelful of hair littered the floor.

But cutting hair wasn't as easy as I'd expected. Deep gouges appeared in some places while other locks stood out too far, like corkscrews. As for the back . . .

"My God, Catherine, what are you doing to yourself? At least let me touch it up. It's so uneven!"

She scolded me lightly as she finished the job. "I told you to leave it down to your shoulders. Now you look like an Italian Harpo Marx."

"Just what I wanted!" I grinned at myself in the mirror. "Thanks Mrs. Russo, thanks a lot."

"Well don't tell anyone I cut your hair," she said. "I don't want to lose business. Those empty spots will grow out eventually. Actually it's kind of cute, makes you look like a little boy."

Everyone made jokes as I swept up the hair and I grinned at them, so delighted was I with this transformation.

"You could insulate a house with it."

"You could stuff a mattress."

"It would make twenty wigs."

"Don't mind them," Mrs. Russo consoled me in a low voice so they would not hear. "All of them would be lucky to have hair like this—good, thick, beautiful Italian hair."

I ran all the way home, happy, happy, happy. I'd taken the first important step and it had worked!

Chapter Fifteen

"What did you do to your hair? Now you really are a monkey."

"Thanks, Ma."

"Don't be sarcastic. Maybe it's not so bad. You cut it yourself?"

"Mrs. Russo fixed it up."

"Turn around. It will have to grow in here and there. I guess Gloria's the beauty of the family, God knows, the only one. Don't feel bad, Catherine. I know plenty of pretty girls who are miserable, lots of homely ones, too, come to think of it. Don't be so sensitive, Catherine. You're not *crying,* are you? Don't you want me to tell you the truth?"

"No. It's dumb to tell people the truth!" I yelled. Once more I ran to my bedroom and slammed the door in her face.

The only thing that mattered was that Miss Alcott like it. The next morning I wore my white sweater and skirt. Naturally my mother was right about it. A layer of grime had grayed it, even though I'd worn it only a few times. I dabbed at a small streak of dirt but it only spread further.

"Take it off. I'll clean it for you," my mother said. She scrubbed the skirt with a soil remover that promised to make it smell of benzine all day. "You shouldn't wear it to school the way it smells," she said.

I wore it anyway.

Would Miss Alcott notice my haircut? I would watch my posture, too, stand tall and straight. I hoped the smell would go out of my clothes by the time school was over, because I was going to see her.

I stood before the closed opaque glass door that led to her office, my heart beating wildly. My outline must have been visible through the glass.

"Come in," she said impatiently and when I entered, she glared at me, obviously annoyed. "If there's anything I can't stand, it's someone loitering behind a door."

"I'm sorry. Shall I go?"

"No, don't bother. What's on your mind, d'Amato? Catherine, is that it?"

"I was just wondering if you wanted posters for the spring concert."

"Oh! It's nice of you to offer, Catherine. Thank you. I'll let you know if we want them."

She stared at my hair, at my white sweater and skirt that so pitifully imitated hers, and I could not tell myself it pleased her. She did not like me. I knew it. It was as simple as that. Nor did she care if I took her beauty program seriously or not. It had been a mistake to come.

But in that last second before I turned to leave, I saw that all six of the posters I had made for the Christmas concert were tacked on the wall. One was torn at the corner and the others showed wear around the edges, but all six were there. So she must have liked them after all!

"Thanks, Miss Alcott," I said, grinning as if she had just heaped a barrel of compliments on my curly monkey head.

Toward the end of January we had the gift of a free day because of a teachers' convention that began on Friday.

As soon as my mother left for work, I opened the living-room window and stood before it, practicing deep breathing while the January air rushed into the house. The winter fog drifted through the streets, softening them and nearly hiding four old women in long, black coats who stopped to chatter briefly before hurrying to the bus stop. Three of these were cleaning women on their way to luxurious houses on the west side and in the suburbs. Careworn and bent, they carried plastic shopping bags and walked as if they were already weary, even though the day was only beginning. Did they ever think about beauty and how anyone could attain it? If they heard Miss Alcott declare it was a seed germinating deep within them, would they laugh? And who could blame them?

But that seed was still within my grasp. All one had to do was *believe*. I practiced long breaths and short breaths to purify my lungs, then sat on the floor to suffer the whole torturous routine of stretching and bending. Possibly I cheated a little, doing each bend only four times instead of ten, but I was thinking about beauty in the deeper sense and how it begins within and works outward "to take place in a harmonious environment," she had said.

As I put back the massive furniture that I'd pushed against one wall to make room for my exercises, I stopped and looked at the apartment as if I'd never seen it before. Ugly! My God, it was ugly. Everything in the world was crammed into that tiny space—castoff furniture, soot-caked drapes, cheap, gaudy lamps, the television that was too large, and the rug, which was maimed by a dark spot that could not be cleaned or covered with furniture since it occupied the center of the room. It had been a gift from Aunt Carol when she moved to the new home in the suburbs.

"I'll fix up the place one of these days," my mother used to promise, but apparently she had given up on the idea. I could hardly blame her; it appeared so hopeless.

If it were up to me, I was thinking, I'd throw everything out, tear down the drapes, clean everything, then paint the walls, the floors and the scratched brown woodwork a pure white. The beds would be only mattresses on the floor covered with serapes or handwoven blankets like those photographed in the art magazines at school. The living-room furniture would consist of one low table where we would take our meals in peaceful conversation or meditative silence as we sat on square cushions, like the Japanese. My mother's houseplants—she had the gift of gardening—would cover the windows instead of curtains and her glorious Boston fern would hang from the ceiling like a piece of sculpture. All against a background of pure whiteness!

How airy and spacious it would become, how liberated! I vowed to do it!

Pulling on my jacket, I ran to the Payless Drugstore just as it was opening. The paint cost more than I had expected, and with even the cheapest paintbrush I had exactly eleven cents left in my wallet. No lunches next week, but what did it matter? You can't be too thin, Miss Alcott had told us.

At home I tied a kerchief around my head, took down paintings, posters, news clippings, sketches, and photos of Tony along with the precious photograph of my grandparents—all of which had covered my bedroom walls. I covered the bed with an old sheet and caused a dust storm as I swept down the yellowish wallpaper.

The first brushful of paint slapped on the wall sang out of the gloom. A few drops fell on the floor and then I remembered to spread newspapers around. But maybe I'd go ahead and paint the floor white, too.

The first wall soon became a fearless white. On the second wall I became Picasso with full sweeps of the brush. A profile. A staring eye. A fleeing nude. A goat. Someday I'd paint murals on walls the size of a barn.

By one o'clock it was done! The four walls, the bureau, the desk, the frame around the wavering mirror, and the chair . . . all transformed into pristine whiteness. After a quick lunch, I covered the living-room floor with newspapers and the furniture with old sheets, since one drop of paint on the ugly sofa or cocoon chair would have spelled THE END for me. And so I began. A surprise for my mother!

That for you, I cried as I covered the first square yard of mottled, decayed brown wallpaper! Bored with an orderly application of paint, I experimented with abstract brushstrokes that turned into nude dancers cutting up wildly. Using the narrow edge of the brush, I gave them monkey faces. Amusing. Later, of course, they would disappear under a covering of solid white.

As I bent down for another brushful of paint, I caught a glimpse of my Timex. Yipes! I should have been at the Mona Lisa ten minutes before. Now Mrs. Russo would scold me and warn me there were hundreds of girls waiting to get a job as good as mine.

I wrapped the brush in wax paper and put the lid on the paint can, which was nearly empty. Had I actually used two gallons of paint? I'd have to buy more then, when I had the money. I flew from the house after one last glance at the living room wall. Good-bye, monkey dancers! Good-bye, beautiful spirits!

Indeed my mother was surprised. I had ignored a persistent sneaking fear that she might be less than happy at first.

"Less than happy" is far too mild an expression. She was fuming when I came home that evening.

"Catherine, what's the big idea? Who told you to paint the walls? White walls? This is *my* apartment; I'm the one that says what will go on here. Where do you get the nerve to do this, without asking? I tell you, when the landlord kicks us out, *you* can go find us another place to live."

"I only wanted to surprise you, Mom."

"Surprise! You did that all right. It would surprise me if you did something right. Can you smell those fumes? You paint in summer, stupid, when you can have the windows open, not in winter."

"It's too long to wait for summer," I mumbled, standing there with my head hanging down, waiting for the twenty-minute lecture which would be sure to follow. I felt like a six-year-old who tried to bake cookies to please her mother (and herself) and burned down the house in the process.

My mother carried on. "If only I had your opportunities. . . . You call this art, these monkeys? Monkeys, why monkeys? You oughtta be grateful you got a roof over your head. . . ."

I assured her I was grateful, I really was, and that I meant to cover the walls completely but ran out of paint, but I'd get more; I'd pay for it myself; she'd see for herself the room would be brighter. No matter, nothing I could say could stop her rampage. I had to wait it out.

"Can you imagine Gloria doing anything as crazy as this? Oh no. Gloria, who doesn't need anything more in this world, *sells* her drawings. Did a thought like that ever enter your mind? Not you. You have to make monkeys on the walls."

"Oh God," I moaned softly so she wouldn't hear me, "I wish I were dead."

But she heard it, changed instantly. "Catherine, you mustn't say that!"

"I didn't really mean it."

"You mustn't ever let the words come out." Then, since she had already accomplished her goal of making me miserable, she softened, reducing her anger to a sermon. "We all want things we can't have. For a long time I wanted big things—a car, a real fur coat, a big house. Now I'm grateful to hang on to my crummy job and this awful apartment, scared I'll lose them."

The room was getting dark and there we sat, verging on tears, half-drunk on self-pity and paint fumes.

"There's no point crying about it," my mother said, blowing her nose.

"I'm not crying," I said, sniffing. Now that she had unburdened herself and the storm was over, for no reason I could think of, everything began to seem funny. The dancers on the wall with their monkey faces were saying that everything was funny; it was all a big joke. Then I began to laugh and couldn't stop. I rolled on the floor until I had to hold my sides.

"Catherine, you're crazy, absolutely loco. What's so funny?" my mother asked, but I only laughed all the harder. At last my mother began to smile. Her tantrum was over.

She was nearly broke, too, but that night we went out to Kentucky Fried Chicken and afterwards to a movie to cheer ourselves up.

If my mother has a saving grace, it is this, that she is unpredictable.

We lived with the monkey dancers for a week. On the following Saturday she called the office of the Wozniak Dress Company and pleaded illness. From the tone of her voice, it sounded as if she were dying, and I told her the girls in the office were probably taking up a collection for the funeral wreath. She grinned with pleasure at the unexpected holiday, poured herself another cup of coffee, and then dressed for a day's work at home. She put on ancient plum-colored pants and a sweatshirt left over from Vincent's high school days, and tied a white kerchief around her head.

"Okay, Catherine, let's get it finished!"

That day she was magnificent. Though she dislikes little bits of housework, she blooms on the occasion of major cleanings. While I painted the living room walls, obliterating the monkey dancers, she repotted her plants. I think they loved her, for they thrived, bloomed, and burgeoned even in that dark, sunless place. My mother scrubbed, cleaned, and polished, all the while singing in a full, lusty voice the songs she had grown up with—the music of Frank Sinatra, Bing Crosby, Rosemary Clooney, and even Elvis.

We argued slightly about the color of the kitchen. She insisted on an ugly mustard yellow. Her bedroom, she said, caressing each word, would be "a soft, glowing rose." Sometimes I wondered about her fantasies. I agreed to the "soft, glowing rose" and of course offered to paint it and in return she let me have my way in the kitchen, gleaming white with a mustard yellow trim.

I begged her to throw out half the furniture. "What, are you crazy? That's good stuff."

"Well, all right," I agreed. After all, it was her apartment.

On Sunday night when everything was finished and the furniture was put back in place, I asked her if she was happy.

"Happy? How would I know if I was happy or not. But I like the apartment better. And it's really clean, too. What about you?"

"I like it better, too," I agreed, not letting on how pleased I was with this victory.

But I was already leaping ahead to thoughts of a studio. Someday a studio.

Chapter Sixteen

January, February, the beginning of March—it was the tired time of year when winter resented the encroachment of spring. The seasons fought, spring moving in with a thaw that melted snow and turned the ground to mud. Winter lashed back with a freeze, leaving the earth in a state of *rigor mortis*. Another thaw, another freeze, a late snow, and so it went.

Everybody was becoming as cheerless as the weather. The exhilaration of a new haircut and freshly painted walls had long since worn off. I stopped drawing, as if I were waiting for a signal to get me moving again. My mother sagged and gained six pounds. It was the temper-flaring time of year.

Even Miss Alcott did not escape. Her first enthusiasm for telling us what we could become had been, in its way, an overture, a hand held out to us although I never got over the feeling that she really could not like most of her students. For that reason, or possibly because she was such a stickler for rules—a minute late meant a demerit of sorts, an extra pink slip taken meant a trip to the principal—she failed to win everyone over. I was sorry for that, for her insistence that we could become more than what we were had brought with it a message of hope. But she became discouraged. Her voice took on a new coolness, edged with undisguised impatience. She had tried and we had failed her.

"Straight backs, straight backs! Are you sixteen or sixty? Must you all chew gum? You, and you, and yes, you over there, get rid of it immediately. You all look like cows, only nature meant for cows to chew their cuds. It wasn't intended for you. Did you know that chewing gum makes a person appear idiotic?

"Well, since you all seem so listless, let's see you do a cow dance. All of you, quick, down on all fours. Pretend you're cows. I want to see you move like cows, chew your cuds. Everyone, move from that corner of the gym to this. One at a time. Move!"

If only she had smiled to show this was a gentle lecture, we could have gone along with it, but she challenged us with fiery aquamarine eyes and a slow beat on the drumhead. Giggling, embarrassed, bored, indifferent, half the girls refused to take one step while the others lumbered on their hands and feet obediently. One by one they rebelled and came back to stand stubbornly until only poor Donna Ricci was moving, awkwardly and alone. She was used to obeying authority and hadn't noticed that the rest of us had rebelled.

And what would Miss Alcott do in the face of this open rebellion? She could not report all of us to the principal without jeopardizing herself. She took care of it quickly enough.

"All right, Donna gets an *A* and everyone else gets an *F*. Donna, you make a first-rate cow."

None of us cared about grades. We would graduate when it was time, no matter what our grades were, so Miss Alcott failed to reach us, but Donna walked back slowly to the corner, tears swelling in her eyes. Weeping, she left the gym to go to the locker room, where I imagine she sat and sobbed. At that moment I detested Miss Alcott for singling out innocent Donna and letting her make a fool of herself. This time I made no excuse for her.

However, now that she had satisfied her anger, her voice softened.

"Let's talk about animals for a few minutes. I'm not being facetious when I say they are nobler than we are. Think about horses, how proud and handsome they are, or deer, how swiftly they run and leap. Sometimes we have traits of certain animals inside us. This time I want to experiment. Each of you choose an animal, any animal you like, and move across the floor in imitation and see if we can guess what it is."

If only she had taken on this tone before, how delightful this exercise would have been, but I kept thinking of Donna's sad experience. The first girls to perform chose to be rabbits, cats, and horses, while most of the girls from Dance Club leaped like deer, but when it came to my turn, Joanna whispered. "Make a monkey. Go ahead."

"What's all the hesitation back there?" Miss Alcott demanded.

Immediately I started out with my old Catherine the Monkey trick. I hopped about, scratched for fleas, ran for one of the climbing ropes that hung from the ceiling and jumped on it, climbing halfway up, where I swung and pretended to eat a banana. Down again, more tricks, more antics, and to my surprise a round of applause broke out. I leaped about with elaborate bows, pretended to catch the flea that had plagued me, and ended with monkey faces. What a ham I was after all!

"Marvelous, d'Amato! You make a perfect monkey. That's very good. Excellent!"

I began to glow. She had noticed me. I had made her laugh! And yet it wasn't her monkey that I wanted to be but something more, a Catherine that she liked and admired.

I tried to laugh when Joanna crossed the floor in imitation of a cockroach which, unfortunately, nobody guessed, but the laugh stuck in my throat.

The next day Joanna was expelled for smoking in the girls' room; at least that was the excuse used. Had it happened to me, I'd have died of shame, but Joanna stood across the street from the school and smoked brazenly, as unconcerned now as before. A red silk scarf was tied jauntily around her neck and she was wearing new caramel-leather high-heeled boots. She waved her hand frantically, calling me to come over and talk with her.

"I can't stand around, Jo. Got to go to work. Want to walk with me?"

"Can't. Someone's coming by to pick me up in a little while. Russo'll forgive you."

She offered me a cigarette which I didn't take. Everything was depressing me, the weather I might say, but mostly it was Miss Alcott. I was so confused, wanting to forget her and not daring.

"I'm worried about you, Cat, because you're still mooning over that cold fish. Why waste your energy? Look how unhappy you are."

"I'm not unhappy," I flared sullenly.

"Yes, you are, pet. You're in love with her."

"You're crazy!"

"Everyone knows it. You forgot your sketchbook in the locker one morning and we all looked at it. Then those drawings over at your house. Have you decided you're gay?"

"Idiot! Of course not. You're all wrong and I won't listen." I began to walk away but she caught up with me.

"I'm sorry, Cat. Forgive, please?" She took on an expression of mock sweetness. "I know *you're* not gay. About Alcott, I can't say. Could be. I don't care what happens to that icicle, but I'm worried about you. She's not going to do you any favors. I think you're headed for trouble."

"Trouble? I haven't done anything."

"Those sketches. You can't get your mind off her, can you? You made a monkey out of yourself for her in more ways than one. What does she do for you?"

"I can't explain. She stands for the kind of life I'd like to have. And she's beautiful. A real dancer. That's it."

"Hopeless, hopeless. Cat, you should be getting out, going to parties, meeting people your own age."

"You sound like my mother."

"God forbid! But that's what I think. Forget Alcott. Let me introduce you to some really nice guys."

"Most guys don't like me, Joanna. I guess I don't have any appeal. And I don't think I'd be right for the ones you know."

"I guess not," she said quietly. The secure mask she usually wore dropped, and I could see that not everything was easy for my cousin. Maybe it would be better if she talked to me about what was hurting her. But she brightened immediately, though falsely, as a small red Porsche came driving up and stopped suddenly in front of us.

"Hey, Mike!" she said brightly to the man who was behind the wheel. "Can we give my cousin a lift? I've been keeping her here and she's got an appointment."

"Sure," he said cordially. Joanna scrambled in next to him and I sat stiffly beside her, admiring the car. Mike was handsome enough and well-dressed, but older . . . at least thirty or more. A very polite man. He left me off at the Mona Lisa and for a few minutes I wondered if I *had* made a mistake in not taking up Joanna's offer at the beginning of the year. It wasn't too late.

"I will give up Karen Alcott," I promised. Joanna was

right. Dreaming of her would get me nowhere. And yet, as I swept up the hair from the floor of the Mona Lisa, I turned on the fantasies of Karen Alcott the way I would turn on a television channel. Soon I was completely lost in daydreams that took me far away from the dingy world of Catherine d'Amato. How could I possibly give that up?

Chapter Seventeen

The next night I was invited to a party.

Naturally my mother made too much of it, calling Aunt Carol and chatting with Aunt Mary about it. Anyone would think she'd been invited.

"Mom, it's only a staff party for the school paper. It's no honor. See, they had to invite me because I contributed drawings. I have to bring potato chips and a dip."

"I'll buy a big bag of chips. I'll make two dips for you, my best dips. What are you going to wear?"

"I don't know. Maybe pants, maybe a skirt. It's no big deal, just a party."

"It seems to me," she said ponderously, as if making a vital decision, "that this is the kind of party where people will dress up. Dressing up is coming back into style. You want to look nice, make the most of your opportunities. Parties are where you meet people, where you have a good time . . ."

The more she went on about it, the sorrier I was that I'd promised to go. What would I do there? What would I talk about if a boy came over to me? The only parties I'd ever gone to were those my relatives gave.

But there *was* a good reason I should go. If I made friends there, and I would try very hard to do that, then I could forget Miss Alcott. That would be the sign that I should give her up.

The next night, about nine, Aunt Carol appeared at our house and placed a Lord & Taylor dress box in my hands.

"Hello, darling." She kissed me lightly on the cheek. "Mother tells me you're going to a party. Perfect! You'll see, one party leads to another and pretty soon you'll be like your mother, a real party-goer. Your mother would get off her deathbed to go to a party, wouldn't you, Bea?"

"Don't put me on my deathbed so soon," my mother said, smiling and excited. "What's in the box?"

"A few things Gloria can't wear anymore because she's grown out of them. She hardly touched them. That girl thinks she's a princess."

"She *is*," I said in a low voice, wanting to open the box but hesitating.

"What's the matter, Catherine? Still too proud?"

"I just wish I had something to give Gloria."

"Save your worry! Gloria takes care of herself. Go ahead, open the box."

Inside the box, nested in a bed of tissue, was a red velvet skirt and a white blouse with a ruffled neck, something I'd seen pictured in teen magazines. It was beautiful but really too fussy for me. I doubted that Gloria had chosen it.

"Try it on. It's adorable. Just your color!"

I rushed to put it on, loving the softness of the velvet and the silky touch of the blouse, but I wondered if all the frills made me look more like a monkey than ever.

"Perfect, it's perfect!" my mother cried.

Aunt Carol agreed, straightening the blouse and flaring out the skirt, clucking like a hen while my mother nodded approval. At last, she said, I was getting some sense in my head. And now that the matter of the dress was settled, they went on to give me advice.

"Do you know how to dance?"

"Sort of," I said doubtfully.

"They teach them in school," my mother said. "Don't you have a gym teacher who gives dancing?"

"In a way."

"The way they dance nowadays, it's not dancing," Aunt Carol said. "What you must remember, Catherine, is when you get there, don't sit in a corner. Let people see you. Smile a lot; you're always too serious. Talk light. Try to laugh."

"Remember, Catherine, it's like a game. If a boy says something, then say something back even if it doesn't make too much sense. Say nice things to everyone. And if someone asks you to dance, then dance. Just go along with it."

"Up to a point," Aunt Carol interrupted, holding up a forefinger. "You should have Gloria to tell you all about this. If a boy wants to go too far, you say no, but you don't get mad about it. Just laugh, say no, but underneath mean it. You understand?"

The rivalry between the two sisters softened and soon they were laughing at themselves, remembering this party and that dance, a strange boyfriend of Mary's, and the time their father sent their brothers to bring them home from a dance because it was eleven o'clock. They sat in the kitchen and drank espresso, becoming girls again, and suddenly I wished I'd been one of their sisters. Their childhood in the country sounded like something out of a book. When I became as old as they were now, it wasn't likely there'd be anything to laugh about, and I had no sister to talk about it with me anyway.

"Can I have some coffee, too?" I asked.

I changed into jeans and a shirt, comfortable as old friends.

For two hours I sat in the tiny kitchen, drinking coffee and nibbling the anise cakes Aunt Carol had brought along. That night the kitchen was cozy and warm with laughter, a glimpse of paradise regained.

In spite of all the well-meant advice I'd received, my social debut was a series of errors. My first mistake was to arrive on time. Nancy, the hostess, stopped blow-drying her hair to let me in, and I wondered if her jeans and shirt meant only that she hadn't yet dressed or if that was what everybody would wear. Immediately the ruffles of my blouse became stupid, looming three times larger than they actually were and the red velvet skirt became ridiculous.

"Make yourself at home," Nancy cried out.

"Here's the chips and dips," I said, giving them to her. She dipped her finger in one of the dips, tasted it, winked to show it was good, and then disappeared with chips and dips, leaving me alone.

She had already put on a pile of records and turned up the volume of the stereo to give the impression that the party was swinging along. Her home was a second-story flat, small but large enough to make me feel uncomfortable. Disregarding Aunt Carol's advice, I found a chair behind a large Boston fern and there I sat, hoping to remain hidden. But almost immediately a small boy who turned out to be Nancy's kid brother, found me and launched into a routine of riddles, jokes, and limericks that probably was thought shocking in the fourth grade. At last two couples came up the stairs into the living room, and although I waited for them to say hello, they were so engrossed in themselves, they began to dance almost immediately, without noticing me.

"Hey, you wanna dance?" the little brother asked me.

"Not right now," I said, wishing he would go away.

Suddenly everyone began to arrive. Rita's voice boomed

up from the bottom of the stairs and then the room was crowded with a dozen people or so. Since I had little to do with any of them, for I handed in a sketch each week and that was all, I knew scarcely anyone. The party sprang into life, literally heating up the room as the noise level grew higher and the hilarity grew louder. Rita, wearing brightly printed jersey pants and a sophisticated shirt, was having what I guessed was a witty conversation with one of the brightest boys in the school. For the first time, I could actually *see* her becoming important someday. I hung at the edge of the party. Now and then I remembered to smile.

"Catherine d'Amato, right?" a boy asked, someone I didn't know. "I always wanted to tell you, those posters you did were neat and the drawings for the *Gazette* are perfect. I'm saving them, you know that?"

A small knot of people gathered around to compliment me on the posters and the ink sketches I did for the *Gazette* and then, as another record began, I was left alone, except for Nancy's little brother, Jimmy, who asked me to dance with him. "Later," I told him.

Nibbling nervously at some salted peanuts that had been set out in a bowl, I wondered how soon I could leave. I knew that I should never have come, should never have been conned into wearing Gloria's leftovers, should never have believed it would work.

Somebody tapped my shoulder, making me jump. I turned around to see a dazzlingly handsome boy. Hollywood handsome, with thick, blond hair and straight, white teeth.

"Why haven't we met before?" he asked and an expression crept over his face to suggest that I was the discovery of a lifetime.

"I wouldn't know," I said. "Have you been around?"

"Just moved from Boston two weeks ago. I'm Eric Powers." Then I knew exactly who he was, that handsome Eric I had dreamed about all last summer, the tall Apollo with the easy, friendly smile. Even the first name was the same!

"And who are you? I've been staring at you all evening. You're not like the others," he said, and the statement became a compliment.

"Catherine d'Amato."

"No kidding! What a beautiful name! Like someone out of the Renaissance. Didn't Leonardo paint someone named Catherine d'Amato?"

"Not exactly," I laughed, impressed since he was not only so handsome but the first person who had ever mentioned da Vinci or any other artist in conversation. I remembered not to get too serious, as Aunt Carol advised.

"Do you like it here so far?"

"Well, it's not exactly Boston, but I guess it will have to be okay for a while. What's there to do around here?"

"Whatever you want to do, I guess."

He lifted his eyebrows and smiled. "Shall we dance, Catherine?"

"Sure."

At first we danced apart like everyone else, and then he tried something new as he grabbed me, held me so close I could hardly breathe, turned me around, and let me go again. I nearly lost my balance but he smiled charmingly, as if he hadn't noticed. At the end he suggested we get some punch.

The punch bowl was set out on the dining-room table, surrounded by dips, snacks, and several six-packs of beer. Eric gave me a glass of punch, took one for himself, and there we stood and talked, a relief for me, since he did most of the talking. He mentioned the school paper he had edited and a sports column he wrote for a newspaper in Boston.

"A real newspaper? That's terrific. Maybe you can do that here," I said. Aunt Carol would have approved.

"That *Gilkie Gazette* could stand some editing. It needs

one heavy red pencil from beginning to end. Might do something about that," he said. He didn't lack self-confidence.

"Catherine, when the party's over, let me walk you home.
We must get to know each other better."

"If you want to . . . I don't live too near . . . I mean, it's
quite a way."

"No problem. We can take a bus. Or a taxi. Or we can
walk. Say, do you like to walk at night, gaze up at the stars?
It seems to me that's what you might like to do."

"Yeah," I answered, wondering how this was going to turn
out. He was not quite the Eric I had imagined, being far
too conceited, but I was hardly in a position to be fussy. It
was miraculous that he seemed to like me.

I was about to ask him what he thought would make the
Gazette better when Nancy interrupted, pulling him away.
"Eric, there's someone you've got to meet!"

"D'you mind, Catherine?" he begged, suggesting he'd be
back as soon as he could. I pretended to study a watercolor
on the wall. But instead I saw reflected in its glass a picture
of Nancy dragging Eric through the crowd, which had grown
considerably. I looked around slowly, careful not to stare
directly and saw Nancy introducing Eric to Ginny Kern, a
good-looking girl, one of the stars of the basketball team. It
didn't matter that she had nothing to do with the school
paper, since all kinds of people were crashing the party. What
did matter was that Eric seemed to be giving her the same
"here-you-are-at-last-how-long-I've-been-waiting-to-meet-you"
attention he had given me, and she was melting. Within
minutes they were dancing. He held her close to him and his
eyes were half-shut as though he were in ecstasy.

So much for Eric, and for all such Erics!

Jimmy, Nancy's brother, found me again, this time with
a new riddle. "What crawls up . . ." he began, but I fled,
careful not to appear in a hurry, to the bedroom, where I

found my jacket at the bottom of the pile on the bed. Should I say goodnight to Nancy, thank her for the party and lie about a headache? Not necessary, I decided.

It was easy to scramble down the stairs and rush into the cold street. The noise of the party grew fainter as I rushed, running and skipping away before settling down to a walk.

In the next few minutes I realized I couldn't go home yet. It was only a few minutes after ten and my mother would be waiting to question me about the party. I dawdled, stopped at a coffee shop for a prolonged cup of coffee, walked homeward slowly. The streetlights were dim, leaving dark stretches of shadows. A drunk lurched along the opposite side of the street and became loudly sick in the gutter.

How I hated that and everything else about my life! I didn't belong anywhere, not in school, not at parties, not at games. My family took me in because they had to. Possibly there was something wrong with me, something missing; I was a defective product that should be tossed on the dump heap. I tried to peer into my future and saw nothing there but myself wandering up and down dark and lonely streets.

I walked slowly, block after block, and soon I slipped back into a familiar dream. Karen Alcott and I, friends now, walked quietly together by the shore of a wide northern lake, sapphire blue under a vast sky. We wanted nothing more than to live in peace together, she with her work, me with mine. If only she understood how deeply I cared for her, and that I was not simply another student but a person who cared, she would begin to discover me. "You really are an artist," she would say.

I longed to hear those words from her lips. All right then, I would go back to my drawings and let them speak for me. No more putting it off, I would finish the portfolio before spring vacation and give it to her. After that, what happened, would happen.

Immediately I felt easier. At least that much was settled.

I arrived home near midnight. To my mother's questions about the party, I answered, "It was beautiful! A good party. I danced with a very handsome boy and everyone loved the dips that you made. They really did."

And that, I felt, should have pleased her.

Chapter Eighteen

After my social failure, I became obsessed with one goal, to finish the portfolio and give it to Miss Alcott. It was the one thing that kept me going. Several times I awoke early in the morning, before dawn, and in those most quiet hours asked myself why I should do such a thing. What could possibly come of it? I knew very well that fantasies were fantasies and that in no way was Miss Alcott going to invite me to live with her. I could not quite admit what I already knew, that she did not like me in spite of the posters that hung in her office and the genuine appreciation for my monkey act. So why take on such a mass of work to say nothing about the expense of materials, for I would use only the best papers and inks I could buy.

"I want her to see me, *to know that I exist,* and that I think she is the most remarkable person I have ever met. That alone will be worth all the work."

That is how I reasoned, but something more I did not realize, that as an artist it was time for me to put together a consistent body of work—in this case, my first portfolio centered on one theme.

Now I began again to go over all the sketches, selecting

drawings from seven sketchbooks; hundreds of quick sketches on brown-paper bags, on napkins from the lunchroom, and in the margins of books; endless watercolors and lithograph drawings on all sizes and kinds of paper. The choices to be made were bewildering, since some of the small, instant sketches contained more promise than the larger drawings. I planned to find twenty-five or thirty of the best sketches, making sure there was a good balance of portraits, group studies, and fantasy drawings, then I'd rework them on a good-quality paper and place them in a portfolio which would have to be designed and made.

Some of the drawings were so bad, I nearly abandoned the project. Yet others, that I had forgotten about, showed up with so much vitality I could get quite excited about them. None of the black drawings I had done for Mr. Everett were acceptable. A lightness began to emerge that was very exciting for me now, just as the darkness had been before. Sometimes I thought I had achieved a real breakthrough, as I discovered that a few lines could suggest all the movement I intended. Thanks to the influence of Karen Alcott and the dance, something new was happening in my drawings. I tried for a lightness I'd never been able to achieve before and it was coming!

Night after night I locked myself in my room to work on the drawings.

"Catherine, are you really doing homework? Your last report card wasn't all that great," my mother yelled at me from the living room.

"Yeah, I'm doing homework. Don't bother me," I called back, making a face at her through the wall. Would she never leave me alone? As if grades mattered. The portfolio was my true work and I wouldn't stop until it was finished.

One night when my mother went out with her bowling

team from the office, I spread the drawings all over the kitchen, on the chairs and on the counter. I needed the space and figured I'd have until ten-thirty to work on them.

"Surprise!"

It was only nine-thirty and there was my mother, home early. I shoved the drawings in a pile but couldn't hide them.

"You're early, Mom."

"We were tired, so we quit. What's all that stuff?"

"Homework, for art class."

She picked up a drawing. "What kind of homework is this? Girls in showers?"

"Motherrrrr! They're just drawings, like life drawings. Didn't I tell you they might have an exhibition of my drawings?" Obviously I hadn't, since the idea popped into my head that minute.

"Not like this, they won't. I remember Mr. Turner, the principal, that puritan. He wouldn't let you show any drawings like these. Remember the troubles I had with him when Vinnie was going to Gilkie High."

"Not all the drawings are like that."

My mother looked them over. "Who's this skinny blonde woman? What is she doing, washing her hair?"

"Of course. She's washing her hair, bending over the basin. See, it makes one graceful curve up her back to her head and then down again with her hair falling."

"But she's naked. Couldn't you at least put a bra on her?"

My mother! Did she have to examine every drawing!

"Catherine, who is this girl, this woman you keep drawing over and over?"

"Miss Alcott, the gym teacher. She's a dancer."

"God help us, you're drawing pictures like that of your *teacher*? You think she's going to like seeing herself washing her hair, leaping around without clothes on, and then this. What's this? Looks like she's drowning."

I snatched the watercolor out of her hand and began to put the drawings in one pile. "Mother," I said severely, "That is only a *fantasy,* a beautiful fantasy. Miss Alcott loves my work. She has all my posters on the wall in back of her desk."

"That's different. Those posters were good, Catherine, real good. I don't know how to say this. Maybe your drawings are Art with a capital *A,* I wouldn't know. But I got a funny feeling about them. If I were you, I wouldn't show them to anybody."

Angry now, I snatched up all the drawings and carried them into the bedroom.

"Hey, Cathy," she called. "Come out of there and have some tea with me. I've got some coffeecake."

It happens every time; let me get angry and she becomes sweet. Well, what did she know about art? I loved my drawings and nothing would stop me from going ahead with my plans.

The fragrance of the heated coffeecake drifted to my bedroom and because I never could resist that sweet bread, I went back to the kitchen. Though my mother was annoying, she had meant well. She poured the tea and said she was glad I had come to sit with her. Then, as I might have expected, she began to babble about Gloria's work and why didn't I do that. If only I tried. . . .

"Mom, what she does is make fashion sketches. I am an *artist.* The difference is that she doesn't draw women the way they are but long and skinny and artificial. That's fashion drawing. I want reality."

"Catherine, her work is good because women like to dream they look like that."

"My dreams are more beautiful, like poems."

"If only I could explain. I like the drawings of the girls when they're dancing and sitting around. They're graceful and nice. But that awful blonde woman ... art is supposed to be pretty, isn't it?"

"No, Mom, art is truth, the truth about what you feel."

"All right, I won't argue. But if I were you, I'd hide some of my feelings. Besides, I think some of the drawings are too light. You can't hardly see them."

I sat stony-faced and stony-hearted.

"Don't be so touchy, Catherine. We won't talk about it anymore, okay? Have another piece of coffeecake."

"No thanks. I don't feel well. I'm going to bed, Mom. Good night."

"Take an aspirin, Catherine. I hope you feel better. Good night."

Headache? My head ached but only with anger. In my room a drawing had fallen to the floor, a sketch of Karen as if she were about to dance with her arms uplifted. A long white skirt gave the effect of fluttering in the wind, though a few lines suggested the body beneath. In the background a snowy expanse of land met a gray sky at the horizon. The colors were somber, except for the tip of a yellow-orange sun barely visible over distant mountains. Everything about the drawing was still, hushed and restrained.

"It's not bad at all," I said defiantly. My mother knew nothing about art, nothing at all. I wouldn't waste my time listening to her.

Soon the drawings and paintings were ready. I wrote a few simple words of dedication in my best script in brown ink on a sheet of heavy, cream-colored paper, *For Karen Alcott from Catherine d'Amato.* And then for the portfolio!

It took considerable hunting to find corrugated cartons whose sides were large and strong enough to be used as the base of the portfolio. The process was time-consuming. It

involved cutting two perfectly matched pieces of board, painting them white on both sides and letting them dry, then
finding a layer of thin quilting cotton to glue to the board.
I covered this with muslin, joining the front and the back.
The final steps involved the cutting, pasting, and careful sewing of silk ivory moiré, an expensive material with shifting
patterns woven into it. When finished, the portfolio opened
and closed smoothly. Narrow ribbons extended on the open
sides to keep the drawings from falling out.

I'd never made anything so elegant!

During those days that it took for the portfolio to dry, I
decided to replace a portrait of Miss Alcott. She was surprisingly difficult to draw, for when I glanced at her, she left me
with a certain impression, but when I examined her features,
I found them irregular. One drawing of her gave the impression of a sleek winter animal, but it emphasized the thin
sharpness of her nose too much. Another drawing repro-
duced her faithfully, but one night as I studied it, its cold
stare made me shiver.

All right then, I would try once more, this time a portrait
in a warm sepia-brown pencil on an oyster-white charcoal
paper. I drew the head lightly, sketched in the eyes and
modeled the left half of her face. Then I went to the kitchen
to make a cup of tea because the take-out Chinese dinner we'd
had that evening left me thirsty. When I returned to my desk,
the eyes in the portrait seemed to seek me out and the model-
ing, though understated, was sufficient. Somehow that half-
finished drawing said more to me than a completed sketch.
So that was what had gone wrong with the other drawings! I
had tried too hard to complete them. Miss Alcott was too
complicated to know; she defied being captured and set down
on paper. This drawing with the intense eyes and enough
suggestion of a finely sculptured head was all I knew of her
really, a quick searching glance.

Pleased with this discovery, I placed the drawings in the portfolio, tied the pale ribbons carefully on the top, bottom, and side, and so went to bed. Content at last because the work was done, I fell asleep easily and happily. Before the week was out, Miss Alcott would receive her gift!

Chapter Nineteen

That Saturday, a chilly day halfway through March, was the day, a holy day. As soon as my mother left for work, I sprang out of bed, took a shower in scalding hot water followed by a purifying cold spray, and rubbed my body roughly with a towel. I was very thin now and felt strong and lithe with all the exercising I had done. Was my posture better now than before? I believed I had grown several inches taller (though when I measured my height, not more than half an inch had been added to it). After a spare breakfast of coffee and dry toast, I dressed in the white sweater and skirt, brushed my hair, and stood in front of the mirror, practicing the drama that would happen when Miss Alcott answered the door.

"Well, what a surprise! Come in, Catherine."

"This is for you!" I would say in a low, refined voice as I gave her the portfolio.

"Your drawings? Oh, I must look at them right away. Do come in."

The second version, affected by the March chill and the threat of a cold, unpleasant drizzle of rain, became more realistic. In this, she accepted the portfolio with a cool thanks, but afterward, when she had seen the drawings, she would telephone me to let me know how wonderful they were and how her roommate, Miss Chapin, thought they should be exhibited in a gallery. From that point on, she would respect me; everything would open up; everything would change.

As I walked down Lily Street, bleaker than ever with a raw wind blowing papers around everywhere, I could not squelch certain doubts. I had thought of giving her the portfolio at school, but she was becoming increasingly short-tempered, like many of the other teachers in spring, and I was afraid to go through with it there. Of course a school decision forbidding students to go to a teacher's house had been established for several years, ever since four boys had attacked a teacher in his own apartment. However, I planned only to ring the bell, give her the portfolio, and leave immediately. Such an innocent act couldn't possibly be considered criminal. And so I looked up the location of Chauncey Circle on a city map in the school library and decided to deliver the drawings there.

I took the bus to Victoria Park, then got off and walked with the portfolio under my arm up Suffolk Avenue, which ran along the ridge of a hill. The houses there belonged to the wealthy old families of the city. Grand old houses on broad lawns, some of them like English houses, white stucco decorated with brown boards in geometric shapes; and others, white colonial homes with shutters and bronze American eagles over the doors; and one particularly impressive house with white columns in front. On all the lawns were huge, spreading trees.

At Quincy Drive I turned west, walking away from the city. Here the houses were newer, but still the homes of the wealthy. The streets and sidewalks were empty, almost as if nobody lived there, but dogs barked as I passed, warning me to keep away. Fortunately they were all locked in their yards, closed in by fences.

After four long blocks I came to Chauncey Circle. At the sight of its wooden sign, half-hidden in the trees at the narrow forbidding entrance, my heart began to beat wildly.

"Go back. It's not too late. Go back, go back, go back!"

What, go back now after all the work I've done? Never. Yet it took courage to walk through the narrow wooded entrance that led to this private circle that obviously did not welcome outsiders. I hesitated at the sight of the landscaped park that filled the inner circle and the quiet expensive homes that rested so smugly on manicured yards. Would a pack of police dogs dash out to tear the intruder to pieces? Would alarm bells ring, calling out the police? Not likely. I'd seen too many television shows. Resolutely, walking neither too fast nor too slow, I entered Chauncey Circle. No police dogs, no alarm bells, no police. Only a chill wintry silence.

Could a gym teacher afford to live in such a luxurious neighborhood? 35 Chauncey Circle was a stately white colonial, 33 a slick modern home, 31 a long, brown house stretched out behind a grove of birches, and 29, a dignified house of white brick behind a spacious lawn. A long, black Lincoln Continental parked in front of it was as polished as a slick ad. As soon as I approached 29, a loud, furious barking broke out from a Great Dane. He was so fierce-looking I believed he would tear me to pieces if he could, but fortunately he was chained to a lamppost in front of the house. However, his barking caused an answering chorus of barks from every house in the circle, as though all the dogs were warning that here was a thief, a trespasser, an intruder. Frightened, I stood still and the barking stopped as suddenly as it began. Only the chatter of birds in the bare branches of the trees broke the morning stillness.

But it was 29½ Chauncey Circle that I wanted. Was there such a place? I was left puzzled until I saw, half-hidden in a bed of ivy, a small sign which pointed toward the rear of number 29, along a curving driveway. I followed it and came upon Miss Alcott's white Triumph and a green sports car which I assumed belonged to her roommate. And then I saw where she lived!

A perfect house! At one time it must have been a coach house, a cozy low-lying building with upright boards painted ivory white, dormer windows, and a dovecote on the roof. Huge trees towered in back of it, yet there was enough space and a low fence to suggest a lovely summer garden with brick walks and a sundial. If only I could live in such a place, I'd ask for nothing more!

But my hands turned to ice and my stomach fluttered with fright at the thought of knocking on the door. I rehearsed exactly what I would do, ring the bell or knock, give the portfolio to anyone who answered, and leave quickly. That would be best. Above all, I would avoid all temptations to stay. Please, God, let it be all right, I prayed. Then I rang the bell.

After some time a man, handsome, not very young but impressive and authoritative like the Lincoln parked in front, opened the door. Directly behind him was the dark-haired woman I supposed was Miss Chapin, in sweater and wool pants.

"Hello, there, what can I do for you?" the man asked pleasantly, bending down a little as though I were a Girl Scout selling cookies or someone with a religious tract.

"Is Miss Alcott here? I have something for her."

"Karen, someone's here to see you," Miss Chapin called out.

"Be there in a minute." How the sound of her voice could set me shaking!

"Please come in. It's cold out there," the man said. From

the small entrance hall where I stood rooted, I caught a glimpse of the living room. Fire in the fireplace. Sofas, weavings on the walls, a grand piano, a coffee table covered carelessly with expensive magazines, and a profusion of cushions on turkey-red window seats in front of windows leaded with many diamond-shaped panes of glass—what heaven it must be to live in such a place!

"Someone to see *me?*" Miss Alcott asked, coming into the hall. She did not see me immediately for she was concentrating on fastening an earring, holding her head to one side. Apparently she was on the verge of going out, for she was dressed in a thin wool suit and her hair was pulled back to form a chignon at the base of her neck. Once her earring was attached, she looked up, then stopped short as she saw me. I could feel her tensing in anger.

"What are you doing here?" she asked brusquely.

"This is for you," I whispered, offering her the portfolio. Since she didn't step forward to take it, the man relieved me of it.

"Come on, Karen, this is a handsome portfolio. Is it a present?" he asked.

"Yes. For Miss Alcott," I said, afraid he would open it.

"D'Amato, are you aware that it's against the rules for you to be here?" Miss Alcott said.

"Yes, I just brought . . ." I mumbled, unable to finish the sentence. I turned to go but the man held me back, putting his hand on my shoulder. "Wait a minute. Karen, let's see what this girl has brought you. Drawings? Can we see them?" he asked me and I remained frozen, unable to say anything.

"Karen, this girl is giving you a gift," Miss Chapin pleaded with her roommate in such a way that it was barely short of an outright scolding for her bad manners.

"She has no right to come to the private home of a teacher and this is a rule. She knows it. She's just like all those kids at Gilkie. They don't know how to follow rules," Miss Alcott said, still angry, a white-faced anger. I wanted to go but again the man held me back.

"Karen, have a heart. We should at least look at them. You don't mind, do you?" he asked me. I did mind but could not speak a word. He had already untied the ribbons and was fingering the drawings while Miss Chapin looked over his shoulder.

"Here's a portrait of you, Karen!" she said, apparently delighted.

"And not bad, either, although somewhat forbidding, the way you look now," the man said as Miss Alcott glared at him. "Nice studies of dancers. Karen, you should see these."

Impatiently Karen took the portfolio from him and riffled through the drawings quickly. "I don't know why you waste your time. You have no talent."

She slammed the portfolio shut, bending some of the drawings in doing so, and rammed it into my arms.

"Now take this mess and leave, d'Amato," she said.

Miss Chapin bit her lip and I knew she was distressed at Miss Alcott's behavior. The man opened the door for me. "Those are very nice drawings, really. Very good. I'm sorry about this but..." he shrugged his shoulders as though he could not help what had happened. I was too shocked to answer.

Once outside in the cold, I came to life, ran down the driveway, across the frozen lawns, and out of Chauncey Circle while the dogs set up a murderous howl. All I knew was that I had to leave, to get away from that place as fast as possible. I ran up Quincy Drive and along a street that led to Victoria Park. My sides were bursting with pain and I could not catch my breath. After ten or twelve blocks I came to the park and in one last spurt reached a grove of birch trees and there I collapsed, lying on the ground, taken over by a sudden fit of dry sobs so deep I was afraid I'd never catch my breath again.

She hates me, she hates me, she hates me. The words repeated themselves again and again. The sobbing stopped and I lay stretched out on the frozen ground, not knowing I was freezing. The time for daydreams was over. She had never liked me and never would. I would have to rub her out of my mind, as if she had never existed. But how?

My poor drawings! "You have no talent." Was that true? Could she be right? I was so sure that I was an artist. Was that an illusion, too, a daydream like the others? If so, then I didn't want to live anymore.

A squirrel stopped ten feet away from me and stared. Blackbirds scrapped in the bare trees above. Were they laughing at me? Sounds of children at play drifted through the silent park and I sat up suddenly, not wanting to be discovered lying down. A teacher or scoutmaster was leading a class down toward the pond. Their caps and jackets were joyfully bright against the somberness of the landscape, and I envied their noisy vigor. Everyone was happy, so happy this morning. I'd change places gladly with any of them—the squirrel, a blackbird, a noisy child.

The children left and suddenly I realized my teeth were chattering, I had become so chilled. With the portfolio still under my arm, I walked to the bus stop and waited there for what could have been a few minutes or hours. I sat on the seat of the bus stiffly, my eyes riveted to the floor until it was time to get off.

Fortunately my mother was not yet home. I stopped in the apartment to get matches, then went out to the incinerator that stood in the rubble-filled backyard of the apartment building. I burned the drawings one by one, knowing that all must go. The flame caught on the corner of each sketch, spread across the page, curled into a bright flame and then died, leaving only an ash. Karen Alcott, the dancers, the portraits, the daydreams, all the brave new drawings that had cost hours of work, turned to ashes in a few minutes. When that was done, I tried to burn the portfolio, but it only became singed and would not catch fire. A cold drizzle began to fall, making a fire impossible, so I threw the portfolio in the ashcan, wanting never to see it again. One of its satin ribbons, hanging over the edge of the can, grew limp in the rain.

Feeling nothing, neither sadness nor relief nor any emotion at all, I went into the house and changed into my work uniform. I sat on a kitchen chair and watched the clock until it was time to go to work, and then I walked to the Mona Lisa mechanically, like a robot, hardly noticing I was getting drenched in the rain. Once during the afternoon as I worked, I caught sight of my face in the mirror. It had become as stiff and unmoving as a mask.

Chapter Twenty

That weekend I turned to lead. I vowed I would never love anyone again, male or female. I was alone in this world and that's the way it would be for a long, long time, perhaps forever.

What was impossible to believe was that in spite of all that had happened, I found myself embarking on still another fantasy with Karen Alcott, but it was only the remains of a habit, like Pavlov's dogs salivating when the bell rang. All fantasies, all feelings, all dreams of her had to be stopped, ended, killed. I ached to see her again and dreaded it at the same time. What would it be like in gym on Monday?

I could have saved myself the agony, for something else happened instead. Half an hour before gym was to begin, I was called to the principal's office and told by the secretary to wait outside. I sat there for twenty minutes, worrying and waiting.

"You may go in now," the secretary announced in the manner of a women's matron in a jail. She left me quaking before the principal, Mr. Turner.

"Catherine d'Amato? Sit down, please. Was Vincent your brother?"

"Yes."

"Ah yes! I remember him well. Trouble, many times. And now it seems I've got trouble with you."

"Trouble . . . with me?"

I began to feel sick. I always prided myself on being good, the opposite of poor Vinnie, and yet here I was. Vinnie's sister.

Mr. Turner, a tall, gaunt man, slender except for the bulge in his stomach which suggested he had swallowed a football, peered down at me through half-glasses. Then he shuffled papers on his desk and made a noisy show of stapling them together, marking some with a red pencil—an effective way of making his victims nervous. Presently he folded his hairy hands and narrowed his eyes in my direction.

"I'm sorry to say I've had a bad report about you. I can't remember that you've ever had disciplinary problems, have you?"

"No, sir."

"Miss Alcott tells me you went over to her house on Saturday morning. Is that right?"

"Yes."

"Why did you go there?"

"To give her some drawings."

"Why?"

"I thought she liked my work. I did some posters for her for the Dance Club Christmas Concert. I had lots of drawings of dancers and . . . that's it."

"Why didn't you give them to her in school?"

That was hard to answer. "I don't know exactly. She was always busy in class and I guess she wanted to go home right after school. Besides, I had to go to work."

"Don't you realize that you broke the rules by going to Miss Alcott's house? That's a very serious offense in this school. Miss Alcott was very upset about it."

I looked down at my hands, not knowing what to say.

"Suppose you tell me about these drawings."

"They were drawings of the girls in Dance Club at rehearsals. A few portraits in ink, charcoal, watercolor. Two in pastel. Miss Alcott gave me permission to draw the girls at rehearsal. A few of Miss Alcott dancing, that's it."

"Are you sure? Miss Alcott was very upset. Could you bring in the drawings and show me?"

"I'm sorry, I can't."

"Why not?"

"Because I burned them up, every one."

"You burned them? Why? It doesn't make sense, does it, to do all that work and then burn it?"

I slumped in the chair, crushed now, my voice reduced to a whisper. "She glanced at them fast, but she wouldn't look at them."

"I see. Tell me, Catherine, did you or do you admire Miss Alcott very much?"

"I did before."

"You thought she was a good teacher, different from the others, something like that?"

"She was—is—a good dancer. For a while she tried to make us think there was hope for us. Then I guess she changed her mind. I don't really know."

My head fell forward and I couldn't say anymore. Mr. Turner leaned back in his chair and his voice became kinder, less like that of a district attorney.

"Catherine, do you have many friends?"

"Not really."

"Then you probably don't go out with people your own age. Do you ever go out with boys?"

"No." I was barely whispering. "Anyway, I'm busy. I work after school and on Saturdays."

"Would you go out with boys if they asked you?"

"I guess so."

"But for the most part you keep to yourself. Is that right? And so when you found somebody you liked, you went overboard a little. Would you say that was how you felt about Miss Alcott?"

It was so ugly coming from him that I couldn't answer. He would never understand the complexity of my feelings.

"Catherine, I want to ask you something in strict confidence. I know you're upset, but I want you to think clearly. This is confidential, remember. What do you think of Miss Alcott as a teacher?"

"She's good in some things—dancing, basketball, gymnastics. She's good but not everybody likes her. I don't think she likes most of the girls. Some of them hate her."

"Come now, that can't be true! I hear she's very popular. Actually she's one of the best gym teachers we've had. Dance Club is giving a spring concert and the basketball team has been winning games, and I hear she's planning a gymnastics demonstration that should be popular. This would seem to prove that she's able to get along with students and her judgment is reliable."

I nodded noncommittally. It no longer mattered to me. A prisoner before the judge, I was waiting for him to pronounce the sentence.

"Catherine, I have bad news for you. You know we have a rule stating that students must keep away from the homes of faculty members. I know your intentions were kind. But Miss Alcott has complained and thinks you should be expelled."

"B-b-but I only wanted to give her a gift."

"I know, but there are rules and they must be obeyed. We can't make exceptions. If we did, you see, everyone would think it's all right to break the regulations. They're there for a purpose."

His lips closed in a hard, tight line, as if he were performing his duty.

"One more matter. Miss Alcott requested that you be excused from gym for the rest of the year. She admitted you worked very hard and you will get a passing grade. That's fair of her, isn't it? You'll be expelled from school for a week and when you come back, you may go to study hall instead of gym. Now then, I'll give you a note you're to give to your mother and during this week I want you to think very carefully about what it means to disobey rules."

The accused could barely stand before the judge. Mr. Turner gave me the note for my mother and dismissed me. Slowly, as if moving underwater, I walked through his office and out through the front door. The school bell rang its harsh release and behind me students were pouring into the halls. I crept home, too numb to think. My father was a loser, my brother was a loser, and now I was a loser, too. My period was beginning and the dull, gripping pains threatened to become worse.

At home I pulled off my shoes and crawled into bed. Shivered. The apartment remained strangely quiet except for inexplicable cracking sounds in the walls and gurglings in the water pipes. At last I fell asleep, but when I woke up, the bitterness of my disgrace had not lessened. Then I remembered I had to go to work. I washed my face, which was white with a greenish tinge, the face of a criminal.

Chapter Twenty-One

On Tuesday morning I dressed reluctantly and sat with my mother in the kitchen. Naturally I had destroyed the note the principal had asked me to give her and pretended I would be going to school as usual. The skies outside threatened more rain and my mother frowned at the weather, then buried herself in the morning papers, and not once did she see me.

"Be good, Cathy. Don't do anything I wouldn't do," she called out as she left.

As soon as I was reasonably sure she was on the bus, well on her way to work, I slipped back into bed, pulled the covers over my head, and prayed I would sleep forever and never wake up.

Now I admired Joanna, who could be so indifferent about being expelled. "So what!" she had said, snapping her fingers. But I wasn't Joanna. Everyone would know I'd been disgraced. Gossip spreads.

Time moved slowly. Always before this, I had begged for enough time to stay home, draw, make cookies, or even sew.

Now, since I could not sleep anymore, I found there was nothing I wanted to do. The newness of the fresh paint had long since worn off, and the apartment was as drab as ever. I no longer cared.

Slowly I picked up a sketchbook and pencil. How sluggishly I moved! What should I draw? Never before in my life had that question arose. Sitting at the table, I drew the still life there—the chipped sugar bowl, the crumpled napkin, my mother's coffee cup with the lipstick smudge where she had pressed it against her lips. The drawing said nothing. I blotted it out with a series of deliberate X's, each one a small murder.

"You have no talent." The words were etched in my brain.

Perhaps brush and ink would work better. Mr. Everett said this was a way of waking up sleeping painters. I mixed ink and water in a small dish and let the brush wander over the paper as it wished. It moved across the page in one horizontal stroke. Thick black strokes followed, horizontal, above and below that first drag of the brush, until the whole page became one black mass, a page of death.

There was nothing more to draw. That page said it all. Blackness without light.

A scrap of moiré left over from the portfolio dropped out of the sketchbook to the floor. I picked it up, then slashed it with scissors, cutting it again and again until it lay shredded and dead.

That done, I put away my brushes, inks, and sketchbook, and wondered if I would ever draw again.

What would I do with my days? I took to walking, but I was no longer free to go anywhere. It was necessary to avoid those streets near the Mona Lisa and the ones near the factory where my mother worked, and I could not walk to the

South End in case I came across Aunt Mary. Never again would I walk west toward Victoria Park or anywhere near Chauncey Circle.

One direction was safe enough, the place where Ravenna Street once stood. On Wednesday I walked downtown and stood in front of the giant towers of tall glass buildings where Front Street and Commercial Street used to be. The shiny surfaces of the buildings reflected other glass buildings and the gray skies beyond. From time to time I caught sight of a small person, head set down into the collar of a peacoat, hands in pockets. A reflection in the glass. So that was me? Never a sadder monkey than now.

Eden was gone, my childhood garden long since murdered. River Street had become a cement highway along which cars and trucks sped, leaving behind a poisonous exhaust. No sidewalks, no place to walk there. The river was hidden from view, as if that too had disappeared.

Leaving it, I walked for several miles in a northerly direction before I realized I was in a part of the city I'd never seen before. Melancholy streets and mean houses. I walked up one side street and down another, as though this were a foreign country. A small child stood on the sidewalk and bawled, but I was so wrapped up in my own misery that I passed him by, then woke up and turned back to kneel beside him. I found a Kleenex in my purse and wiped away the snot and tears from his face. I put my arm around him.

"There, it's not so bad, is it? Where do you live?" I asked.

He pointed to a dismal brick house in a yard full of gravel and weeds. An obese woman stared through the curtain and then waddled out of the house to yell at me.

"Whadya think yer doin'?" She grasped the child roughly, stabbed me with a hostile look, and pulled her son into the house.

Now he knows what it's all about, I thought. Poor kid, to learn so soon.

"Are you feeling all right? You're pale," Mrs. Russo said.

"I'm fine," I said, forcing a smile. "School's a bore, but that's nothing new."

That remark was meant to keep her from becoming suspicious and perhaps asking my mother about me. Her eyes narrowed as if something were not quite right, but someone called her away and I suppose she forgot about it.

My mother could have been suspicious. "Don't you feel good, Catherine? I hope you're not dieting. You're much too thin now. You hardly ate anything."

"I don't know. I guess I'm not hungry."

She leaped for an answer. "It's your period, isn't it? I used to have a bad time with it, too. No wonder they called it 'the curse' when I was growing up. You want to go to bed?"

"If you don't mind." I was well past the point of pain, yet I craved bed, the best place of all right now—safe, dark, and warm. I burrowed beneath the covers and wanted to stay there forever. Yet when I dozed off, the nightmares came. Again and again I relived the trip to Chauncey Circle, saw Miss Alcott fixing her earring and then the wrath on her face. I heard her voice, low and chilled, heard her scream at me. As I fled across endless frozen lawns, dogs barked and I was shot in the back again and again until I dropped dead. I would wake up shaking, then fall back asleep, only to go through the same dream again.

Wouldn't it be better to be dead after all? Death was peace. Rest in peace. Again I saw Ed Magill as he lay in his coffin, so tranquil, so calm.

It wouldn't be so hard to die. A few minutes of pain, of course, but what a small price to pay for eternal peace. Never more would I have to worry about anything—my monkey face, my lack of talent, my mother's scolding. I could cheat the rotten future that faced me.

If only I could die . . .

I buried myself deeper under the covers and this time slept dreamlessly, a temporary death.

On Friday it poured. I visited the museum for the third time that week, stood in front of a dozen paintings and failed to see one.

I had hope that Joanna would call me. What a relief it would be to see her and tell her everything that had happened! It came to this, that she was the only one I could talk to openly. She would scold, of course, and let me know what an idiot I'd been, but then too she would revive me. But she didn't call me and I didn't have the heart to call her.

Nobody called. I was abandoned. Completely forgotten.

At home once more, I cleaned my room, straightened out the closet, putting Gloria's clothes on one side and mine on the other. I destroyed a diary I had once kept. With a blood-curdling rip of paper, I tore down the poster of that Norwegian seaport I had decided was Miss Alcott's spiritual home and placed it in the ashcan outside, along with worn-out shoes and some cheap jewelry that Joanna had lifted from a drugstore and later given to me.

But there were those things I could not possibly destroy. Ed Magill's print of the toad with the pleading eyes, the sketch I'd done of Aunt Mary and her children, a photograph Tony had given me and that other photograph of my grandparents. I left them on my desk.

Was it possible to erase a life as though it were a badly drawn sketch? Would I be given another piece of spotless paper? Could I begin again?

The somber newsprint portrait of the six-year-old Catherine gazed at me with surprised eyes. I could not meet her crayoned glance, "that one who has a gift." I left her on the wall untouched.

Then I sat down on a straight-backed chair in my chastened room. Very calm I was now. I had decided that I would not live to see my seventeenth birthday, but when had it happened? In front of Ed Magill's coffin with the ribbon that promised REST IN PEACE as a reward for dying? When I ran from 29½ Chauncey Circle? When I saw what my father had become? When I wiped the tears of the sobbing little boy and saw him being pulled away by the dreadful woman who was his mother?

I got up and saw myself in the mirror. There was the reason, looking back at me soberly. Catherine herself.

I was feeling a sad heaviness, yet I had never experienced such relief. My decision was made. I tried to imagine what it would be like to be buried in the earth, below the roots. It would be very dark, very still, very cool. Never would I have to weep or laugh again.

I hoped that my mother, who had such a way with plants, would grow a garden on my grave—primroses, daisies, and poppies.

On Saturday night my mother was invited to a party at Aunt Carol's, presumably to meet the perfect man my aunt had found for her. A family of matchmakers if ever I saw one.

"I hate to leave you alone, Catherine. What about if you go to the movies? I'll treat you."

"Thanks, Mom, but I don't mind staying home. I've got this good book I want to read."

"You're sixteen and you stay home with a book on Saturday night! You're something else. Wish you didn't look so pale. I tell you, I'll get home early. Would you mind zipping me up the back?"

She chattered while I struggled to pull the zipper up over

her fleshy back. At one time I would have despised the loud print of her dress, pink and red roses against a black background, but now its too-bright colors and sleazy shine, along with her red shoes and the jeweled butterfly she placed amid her soft auburn waves, spoke another message—that she loved being alive.

She hummed as I combed out her hair and refastened the butterfly ornament, and smiled at herself in the mirror as I clasped an imitation crystal necklace at the back of her neck. That night she became one big gaudy flower.

"Mom, maybe you really will meet the right guy. Do you think you'll get married again?" I asked.

"How should I know? Maybe, if I meet someone."

"It could happen. Don't be too fussy. I hope you have a good time tonight, Mom."

"You know me, Cath. One glass of wine and I'm ready to have a wonderful time. You're sure you don't mind if I leave you, do you?"

"Mom, what's all this worrying? It's okay. Please go. Have a good time. Say hello to Aunt Carol for me."

She puttered around, putting on last bits of make-up and perfume, and at last she was ready to go. I stood by the door and rather hoped she would kiss me goodnight, as she sometimes did, but she was probably afraid of smudging her lipstick. She patted my cheek a little and promised not to stay out too late.

Her heels tapped down the corridor and the outside door clicked behind her. Then I locked the door of the living room and welcomed my last Saturday night.

After she left, peace and excitement, that heady mixture, swelled within me. Perhaps I've been compulsively neat all along, I decided, as I straightened out the living room, fluffing up the pillows of the sofa, although they were too weary to be fluffed up much, piling up the magazines my mother had let fall beside her chair, and straightening for the thousandth time a picture on the wall that couldn't hang straight —a sepia watercolor of Naples. At the same time another Catherine seemed to be hovering above it all, watching myself doing those things.

I gave my mother a gift of order as I hung up in her closet those clothes she had dropped on the bed and chair. I remade her rumpled bed, wiped off the top of her bureau, where loose powder and traces of make-up had caked, and there I hesitated before a framed snapshot of my mother taken ten years before when we lived on Ravenna Street. How pretty my mother was then, how young, showing the same vitality she took on now only once in a while, as when she went to a party! A tiny Catherine stood beside her. What a serious child, with enormous eyes and a head full of dark curls!

("Catherine d'Amato, could you possibly kill that child?")

I decided that was ancient history, something that had happened long ago. The child had become something else.

My room had been stripped of excess things, clothes and papers, and now it stood in ordered sterility. Those sketchbooks I had not yet used were piled neatly on my desk, sharpened pencils stood upright in an amber glass, pens and inks were perfectly aligned. I wondered if my mother would give them to Gloria. I could not quite believe the unnatural neatness, for when I worked nothing mattered but what was in front of me. Papers could be scattered over the floor and my clothes thrown across the bed. Disturbing.

Well then, everything was ready. Why hesitate?

Then again, why hurry? At the last minute, I longed to go outside. Would there be time? Now I had to count the last hours, the last minutes.

A farewell walk down Lily Street took me past a loud Saturday night party with lights, rock music, and hilarity

flowing into the street. A gang of high school students ca-
reened down the middle of the street. One of the boys pretended to stagger and a girl was singing loudly, everyone
drunk.

"Hey, you, whoever you are, whyn't you come along with
us?" a boy called out to me in a slurred voice.

"Sure, c'mon, c'mon. Plen'y o' room. We're havin' good
time, ain't we!"

I hesitated, tempted. Maybe that would be best, to go out
and get thoroughly drunk. It would be easier that way. And
yet I answered something else.

"Thanks a lot. Not now ... some other time."

Would those be my last words then, "some other time"?
Maybe I'd be born again, reincarnated. I didn't know but I'd
find out.

Lily Street ended and I turned left on the street that led to
the church. Then I changed my mind because I didn't dare
walk past the church, and so I ran down a small alley to
another street, a dark, empty street. When I threw back my
head, I could see that the sky was filled with stars, winking,
sparkling, and lighting up the sky. Was that heaven there?
If so, too bad for me. I'd never make it.

Time was ticking by. Never again would I walk up Lily
Street, let myself into the apartment and lock the front door.
I moved easily, like an actress in a well-rehearsed play. Only
my heart was thumping crazily. I might die of a heart attack.

One detail was almost forgotten. I took what money I had,
twenty-two dollars, put it in an envelope, and wrote a note
to my mother. "Dear Mother, I wish there were more of this
for you. Love, Catherine."

Then I proceeded with the long hot bath, a tender rub
with a clean towel, and the luxury of my best and nearly
new nightgown, white cotton with tucks and a touch of em-
broidery. I brushed my hair, studied myself for one last time

before the mirror and then took a new razor blade from the supply my mother kept in the medicine chest and knelt beside the tub.

"Forgive me for what I'm going to do."

My heartbeat grew loud once more, seeming to fill the bathroom with its drumlike sound. I hesitated, then, holding the blade in my left hand, slashed my right wrist. I cried out with the pain of it but remained in control. Taking the blade in my right hand, I slashed my left wrist more effectively, making a deeper cut. I waited to die, but only a trickle of blood oozed out and then stopped. It had to be done again.

Couldn't I do anything right?

Determined to make it work this time, I cut each wrist again, more successfully as blood spurted out into the tub, where it spread in red swirls, staining the water. How richly red it was, warm and fast-flowing! I'd never known how much of it I had.

My head rested on my forearm. Now I lay me down to sleep . . . I was beginning to feel lighter and a strange humming sounded in my ears. Though my eyes were closed, vibrating circles of light kept moving forward and back; it had been exactly the same when I was given ether for a tonsil operation as a child. Then I was retreating, being drawn back into a narrowing tunnel and everything was growing dark.

"Stop!" I cried. I wanted to get back to the light or else I'd die! I tried to draw my hands from the tub but I didn't have the strength.

"Mother of God, help me!"

A wash of black watery paint covered my eyes, my head, my feet. Stroke after stroke of black wound around me until an inky blackness covered everything, surrounding me on all sides, as impenetrable as the walls of a coffin.

Chapter Twenty-Two

Shortly after midnight, I found out later, my mother came home from the party "only slightly mellow," as she put it, after a few drinks. First she kicked off the exotic red shoes which were killing her, leaving them in the living room. She hobbled into the bedroom, took off her coat and loosened her dress with great relief. "Then I saw the bathroom light was on, and I wasn't exactly worried about it, Catherine, so I didn't hurry, but when I did go in and saw you by the bathtub, what a shock it was! I could have fainted, but first I had to rush over and see that you were still alive. Thank God, you were breathing."

She had then felt my heart beating slowly. She kept calling me but I didn't hear. My wrists hung limply over the tub, now full of reddened water, but I couldn't have cut to mortal depth, because they were no longer bleeding. There was blood everywhere, she said, something I could not understand. She held me close to her and I recalled that before I came out of the blackness, I was aware of her body warmth and that familiar smell of her skin fragrance mingled with the powder that she always used.

"Catherine, why did you do it? How could you? Tell me

you're all right, Catherine, please. Tell me ..."

I was rising out of the blackness to a light that was too strong. Her arms holding me, the fragrance of perfume, the smell of wine on her breath ... if I was aware of such things, did it mean then I was alive? Yes, I was still alive. Gratefully I sank back into a dimness.

Sitting on the edge of the tub, my mother held me in her arms as though I were a baby and rocked me back and forth, moaning now. "*Cara, cara,* my baby, my little Catherine." Her eyes filled with tears that mingled with the mascara and rolled down her cheeks.

I pulled myself out of the dimness, since she was smothering me in her arms. "Mamma, it's all right. Don't cry."

"What happened, baby? Thank God. You're alive. Don't talk yet. You're too weak. Let me bandage your wrists and get you to bed."

Too weak to sit up, I leaned against her while she washed my bloodied face and bandaged my wrists with two strips from a clean old towel. My nightgown was covered with blood and how my ankles had also become reddened, I couldn't tell. My mother soothed me with comforting noises while she cleaned me with a warm washcloth and helped me into a fresh nightgown. Leaning on her, I walked to my bed and lay there shivering while she covered me with blankets.

"Are you all right? Comfortable? Shall I call the doctor?"

"No, Mom. No doctor. Please. Nobody must know. But I'm cold." In spite of all the blankets, my teeth were chattering.

"I'll get you something warm to drink. Milk with honey? Maybe a little whiskey first. It's good for you at a time like this."

She held me while I drank the fiery stuff. It burned, but afterward I did not shiver so much. Then she brought me a mug of warm milk with a generous tablespoon of honey dissolved in it, my childhood solace. She propped me up, sat at the edge of the bed and held the mug to my lips, for my wrists were too weak.

"Drink it. It will help. A little more now." She was coaxing me as if I were a baby. I was aching everywhere and could not talk, but she was bringing me back to life. She loved me then. I knew it as I'd never known it before. After a while I finished the milk.

"Good girl. Do you want to sleep now, Catherine? You're sure you don't want a doctor?"

"No doctor. No, Mom. Just stay with me, will you?"

Unaccountably I began to shiver violently and could not stop. It was impossible to explain that where I had just traveled it was unspeakably cold and black. My mother held me and the shivering subsided.

"Don't be afraid. I'm here. I won't leave you."

"Thanks, Mamma," my voice mewed weakly. I fell asleep, then woke up. She was still there. "I'm still alive?"

"Yeah. I'm so grateful. But I don't understand. Why did you do it, Catherine? It's a dreadful sin, the very worst."

"I don't know. It would be better if I were out of the way. Vince could live with you. You'd be free to get married."

"Of all the craziness. If I wanted to get married, I'd get married. That's all. But that's not the real reason, is it. You want to tell me?"

"No."

"Are you pregnant? If you are, tell me, tell me now. It's terrible but it's not the worst thing in the world. At least you're alive."

"No, Mother. Of course that's not it."

"That's a relief. But something happened. What?"

"I can't." I was weeping and I was too weak to cry.

"Catherine," she said sternly. "You mustn't keep it bottled up. It can't be so bad. So tell me, get rid of it, whatever it is."

"I was expelled from school for a week."

"You expelled? I can't believe it. You're always so good. What happened? Did that Joanna get you into trouble?"

"No, she had nothing to do with it. Something else."

My mother's eyes narrowed as she tried to think of the answer, as if this were a guessing game on a TV game show. "Wait, I bet it had something to do with those pictures you drew, didn't it?"

I didn't deny it but began to weep again.

"That woman, that gym teacher. I could tell by your drawing that she was a mean one. I knew those pictures would get you in trouble. She was the one that got you expelled, I'll bet, the one you like so much."

"I don't like her at all. She's a cold, dreadful person. I brought the drawings over to her house to give them to her . . . and she hardly looked at them and said I didn't have any talent. Then I took them home and burned them. And she told the principal I went to her house and should be expelled."

The words jerked and erupted like so much vomit, leaving me drained and shivering again. My wrists ached as if they would fall off. My mother's eyes never left me and I could see her puffing up with anger.

"That bitch! I'd like to give her a piece of my mind. I think I *will,* too. And saying you have no talent! Why, didn't Miss Bowen and Sister Angela back in first grade say that you had a real gift? First thing Monday morning I'm going to that school and tell that principal a thing or two. . . ."

"No, Mom, no! Don't. Please. Everyone will know and you'll only make it worse for me. Please, Mom."

"Maybe you're right," she said, calming down. "But what they did was terrible, awful. You've never been a bad girl. What I can't understand is why you should like a teacher so much, especially that one, but still it's no crime. Did you tell me everything?"

"Yeah, Mamma. Everything. Mom, there's no point in my staying alive. I can't draw like Gloria; I can't type, just can't; I'm no good at parties. What will become of me? Why go on?" My voice was hurting as much as my wrists.

"You mustn't talk like that. There's always a place for everyone and you just go on ... because that's what you do. You go on. You don't stop because some nasty teacher, probably a bitter old maid, or that rotten principal says and does things they have no business saying or doing. You've got to fight people like that, not give in to them."

She put her arms around me, rocked me back and forth.

"Catherine, what would I do without you? My God, what would I do without you? Promise me, you won't ever try it again, not ever."

Love was coming from her in waves, flowing around me, enveloping me.

"It was so cold to be dying. So dark and alone. Mama, I was so alone."

"I know, but you're not alone now, *cara,* and you're alive."

She released me so that I lay back against the pillows, my bandaged hands resting limply over my breasts.

"I'll stay with you until you fall asleep," she promised, and this time I knew that my mother, my big mother, my good mother, would not leave me. Sure of that, I fell into a dreamless sleep.

Chapter Twenty-Three

Twice during the night I awoke and each time I was seized by the trembling fear that I was dead. Then the dim light my mother had left burning in the kitchen so that I would not wake up in total darkness assured me that I was still alive. Relieved, I fell asleep again.

The third time I opened my eyes, the morning was half gone. Sunlight seeped into the room around the edges of the window shade. The six-year-old Catherine d'Amato stared down at me with her carefully eyelash-laden eyes as if to say good morning. The sketchbooks neatly piled on the desk and even the warm blankets that covered the bed told me dumbly of their devotion. The fragrance of Sunday morning coffee urged me to get up, but when I moved, my wrists ached. How they hurt! Why had I abused them so?

Standing at the door of the kitchen, I watched my mother sitting at the table with the Sunday papers scattered all around, sloppiness as usual. This kind of mess had always annoyed me before, but no longer. It seemed that even the clutter was part of life. Besides, newspapers could be gathered neatly and dirty dishes could be washed.

"Catherine, you're up!"

My mother got up from the table and put her arms around me, as if she were really glad I was alive. Why had we never been this way before? I wondered.

"Mom, you don't have to hold me. I'm not exactly an invalid."

"I know, but sit down anyway. I'll get your bathrobe for you. You mustn't catch cold."

How she took care of me, my Ravenna Street mother, watching over her child, bringing me my robe, clearing the table and setting out place mats and the "good" dishes. She stood at the stove, fried bacon, cracked two eggs and let the golden yolks and viscous whites pour into the sizzling grease.

"Eat, Catherine. You need strength. You're too thin," she said, filling my plate and buttering a roll for me. She opened a jar of blackberry jam and set it on the table.

"It's good, but I can't eat so much."

"Eat. After what you did last night, I should be scolding you, but to tell you the truth I don't know what to do. I should shake you by your shoulders for doing such a terrible thing, but I'm so glad to have you alive, I feel like heaven gave me a gift because you're here."

I pricked the egg yolk with a fork and watched the yellow, color of the sun in winter, spill over the whites.

"I still think I'll go up to that awful woman and let her know she practically drove you to your death."

"No, Mom! Stay out of it. Please. Anyway, I'll never see her again. I'm not supposed to go back to gym anymore this year."

"And that breaks your heart," she said ironically. For the first time I wondered if perhaps my mother, my poor fat mother, had been jealous of Karen Alcott.

"I've been worrying about other things, Catherine. Do you think we should take you to a doctor? I didn't even think about an ambulance last night; you'd stopped bleeding, so I figured you were okay then. You want a doctor?"

"No. What could a doctor do? Besides charging you twenty-five dollars, I mean. I don't want a doctor. He'd have to report it and then it would go in the newspapers and social workers would snoop around and *everyone would know.*"

"Then that's settled. But one thing isn't. Catherine, you'll have to go to confession. It's a long time since you've even gone to church, but you can't ignore this. It's a grave sin to take your own life, or to try to take it."

"I know, Mom. I'll never do it again. No way."

"If only you'd talked everything out with me, then your troubles wouldn't have built up. I'm your mother. I'd have listened."

An illusion that. She had never listened. She had only lectured.

"Promise me you'll go to confession?"

"Do I have to?"

"Of course. You don't want to go to hell, do you?"

I wasn't sure if she really believed in heaven or hell, but I could not argue.

"God gives you life and you insult Him when you try to kill it," she said.

"All right, Mother. I'll go to confession."

"Good girl! You'll be better for it. You'll see."

She could not know how I dreaded it. Would I have to tell everything? It was not only my poor gashed wrists that ached. My soul was slashed and bleeding, too. My wrist wounds would heal before my spirit would. A self-portrait would show an angry red cut from the middle of my head down through my body to the center of each finger and toe. I was bleeding everywhere.

My mother poured the last few drops of hot coffee into my cup and my eyes strayed to the corner of the newspaper. March twenty-first.

"The first day of spring," I murmured and then clapped my hand over my mouth, my wrist aching crazily because of it. "Tony's concert! It's today!" How could I have forgotten? My faithlessness shocked me, another sin.

"You're right. I forgot. And he sent us that beautiful invitation."

"We've got to go. He'd never forget it if we didn't."

"But how can you go? You're so weak, so pale. And what'll we do about your wrists? You wouldn't want them to know about it, would you?"

"No, of course not. But we *have* to hear Tony. I'll wear a shirt with long sleeves. Nobody will know."

"You look so white."

"I'm all right, Mom." Actually I was ready to fall over.

She pushed the dishes away and washed my wrists in a basin of warm water that revived my cool fingers and cleaned away the dried blood.

"You should be a nurse, Mom. You have such a gentle touch."

"Sure, sure!" She tied a gauze bandage around my wrists and walked with me to the bed so I could have a long rest until it was time to get dressed and leave. From time to time I heard my mother's voice on the phone or the sound of a crying child somewhere in the building. I drifted in and out of sleep.

At two o'clock, my mother woke me. Was I well enough to go? She brought me a bowl of hot tomato soup and afterward insisted on helping me get dressed. Never before had she been such a good friend.

Snellgrove Auditorium had always impressed me with the grandeur of its size and the importance of its concerts as well as the once-modern murals on the inside walls, lavish with gold paint depicting Apollo and goddesses and nymphs. But we could not go inside yet. Hundreds of people were milling around outside, among them the Martini family, which was gathering, yoo-hooing, and grinning every time another member showed up.

"Everyone's coming. Even Uncle Enrico and Aunt Louise came all the way from Rochester. Isn't that wonderful? Family, that's family."

"Act as if everything is normal," my mother whispered to me unnecessarily. Then, smiling widely, she dragged me over to pay respects to my grandmother and grandfather, who had come in from the country for this family honor. Remnants of stiffness remained between my mother and her parents, but I kissed them warmly. I loved seeing them all dressed up.

"Why you never come to see us, Caterina?" my grandmother asked, hurt that I'd stayed away for such a long time, and I regretted it, too.

"I'll come this summer," I promised them. This time I meant it.

My cousin Rocco, one of the ushers, made his way through the crowd milling around outside to tell us it was time to be seated. Proudly he led us down the aisle to the first four rows that had been ribboned off for Anthony's family. Uncle John and Aunt Flora, radiant in new clothes and already seated, received the congratulations of the family like a king and queen accepting homage due them.

"Who would have guessed it," my aunt Carol said once we were seated, too far away for Tony's parents to hear. "We always used to feel so sorry for John and Flora with that two-bit shoe-repair shop of theirs, the worst business in the family, a penny here, a penny there. They were even too poor to have a store on Front Street. So look what happened! They didn't have to move and now it turns out they're the ones with the genius, a winner like Tony."

For the first time in weeks, I was able to smile, glad that

Tony was the hero of the family and not anyone else. I was happy for his parents, too.

"Is something wrong with Catherine? She's so pale," I heard Aunt Carol whisper to my mother, as if I weren't there or as if I were deaf.

"It could be the flu or something, that's all," my mother said.

The seats were filling up. My cousins sat in back of me and I regretted the childish white shirt I had to wear because its sleeves were long enough to hide my wrists. Joanna in an acid green outfit with too tight a skirt swept in before the concert began and waved at me, wiggling her fingers back and forth. Her mother, nearly transparent with pallor, limped behind her and Aunt Carol whispered what a miracle it was that she had been able to leave the hospital when everyone had expected we'd be attending her funeral.

"She'll outlive us all, wait and see," Aunt Carol predicted, talking lightly of life and death.

Aunt Mary, quite pregnant now, insisted on changing seats with her husband so she could sit next to her "little love, Cathy." "When are you gonna come see us again? The kids keep asking for you all the time. You just don't know how much Bianca loves you. She always puts in a God bless when she says her prayers . . ."

She was going on and on, and I wished she would quiet down because my head was getting light again, but I could see in her eyes that she loved me. How could I have forgotten it? Now it seemed miraculous that anyone could care as much.

The orchestra walked on stage and tuned up, the lights dimmed, and at last I could close my eyes and lean back. A burst of applause greeted the conductor and everyone listened intently to the warm tones of a Haydn symphony; everyone, that is except Uncle Enrico and Aunt Louise, who chatted all the way through. It was as though the orchestra didn't matter, since it was Anthony they had come to see.

At last Anthony walked onstage and nodded professionally to the applauding audience. My cousin had metamorphosed into a young man, far taller onstage than off, more solid and stronger than I'd ever realized. His green eyes swept over the auditorium and then rested on his violin while the orchestra began and he waited for his entrance.

The tones of the violin flowed through the hall. Had I never listened to music before that it should now seem so miraculous? The music was warming me, healing me, bringing me back from the dead. Yes, I was grateful to be alive again, for this, for many things.

As the concerto finished its journey through its early fugue, the gravity of a slow movement, and the final triumphant dance, I stood up with the rest of the audience to applaud and to cheer. Hundreds of people were loving Tony, praising him, thanking him and crying for an encore. Painful though it was, I applauded too, unaware that the buttons of my cuffs had come undone and had slipped back. Too late I realized that Aunt Mary had seen the gauze bandages. When we sat down again, she whispered, "Catherine, your wrists! What happened?"

The lies I'd armed myself with, such as that I'd burned my wrists on the hot iron or had a mysterious rash, proved useless. I couldn't say anything. Besides, she knew immediately without having to be told, and now everyone would know. Catherine, the disgrace of the family.

"You didn't? . . . Oh Catherine, how could you? It's a sin, a dreadful sin. What happened?"

"Shh." Anthony raised his violin to play an encore. This kept Aunt Mary quiet, but as soon as the intermission came, I turned to her.

"It's not what you think. It was just an accident. Please

don't tell anyone, Aunt Mary. I can't talk about it."

Nevertheless, she made reproving clucking noises as she insisted on pinning my cuffs securely with the safety pins she always carried around with her, because "you never know when you'll need them." It was obvious that although she wanted to comfort me, her fingers were shaking, she was that upset.

"I'll pray for you," she whispered.

After the concert the backstage was flooded with Tony's friends and his relatives from both sides of his family, and the air was thick with pride. My mother never left me for a minute, her hand holding mine firmly, as if her little girl could get lost in the crowd.

"You're getting white. Should we go? You could call Tony tomorrow," she said.

I was pushed against the wall and the room was beginning to swim, yet I wanted to stay. Anthony was receiving congratulations like a knight who had been triumphant in combat. If I were drawing, that's how I'd picture him, with his long bent nose and the eyes shining like green pools.

Suddenly he caught sight of me, pardoned himself and made his way through the crowd to where I stood.

"Anthony!"

He hugged me, kissed me. Somebody applauded, as if I were the fair lady receiving his rose, although of course that wasn't the case at all. He read the adoration in my eyes. Then the others claimed his attention.

At home my mother talked of the reception which would take place that night. "Where John and Flora found the money for it, I'll never know, but that's how they are, want to give the family a good time, celebrate when they can."

My mother, who could never resist a party, said we needn't

go if I felt too weak. Possibly it was the first time that I thought of her and how she needed to be with her family at this time.

"I feel fine," I said, lying.

I rested for a while and later we went to the celebration dinner in a South End Italian restaurant, with its palms, accordion player, and tables decked with snowy tablecloths and bottles of wine. Twenty-four hours before this I believed I was at the end of my life. Now as I saw Tony sitting at the head table with his proud parents, and all my relatives celebrating, I felt a surge of love and gratitude that I was still alive.

Chapter Twenty-Four

Monday morning was the hard fact after the headiness of Sunday.

"Are you well enough to go to school? I'd hate to leave you home alone," my mother said. I knew she did not trust me not to make a better attempt at doing myself in.

"You don't have to worry, Mom," I said. "I promised never again and I meant it." What worried me was that everyone would know I'd been expelled and maybe, if Miss Alcott, in her anger, had told them the reason, they would know everything. If my slash-ugly wrists were discovered, then the gossip would be unbearable.

My mother, pinning the sleeves of my shirt so the cuffs would remain securely in place, spouted advice. "If you feel sick, go to the school nurse and she'll let you lie down. Mrs. Russo won't mind if you take off a day from the Mona Lisa. And remember, confession!"

I agreed amiably, fearing she'd repeat the lecture several times over, but this time she hugged me before she left for work and later I set out for school.

I had worried for nothing. Hardly anyone noticed I'd been gone. Of course the teachers knew, but only Mr. Everett mentioned it.

"Welcome back, Catherine. We missed you," he said, being very kind.

"I missed you, too," I said politely, but a second later I realized how true it was. The drawing tables, the smell of paper and chalk, the color wheels displayed on the walls, and even Mr. Everett himself, with his thinning hair combed back carefully over a growing bald spot, touched me unexpectedly, as if I had been very far away from these familiar things for a long time. But I was far from healed, as I was to discover.

"Okay, everyone, a new assignment!" Mr. Everett said cheerfully, hoping that at least three or four students would hear him, for everyone else was talking. "We're going to look out of the window, which is what most of you are doing anyway—I guess it's spring fever time—and I want you to draw what you see. We're lucky to be on the second floor because it's more unusual than the view we'd get on the first. Let's get it done by the end of the hour."

The view offered the swelling buds and boughs of an oak tree, the pink brick of apartments across the street, and on the sidewalks below, a cluster of students loitering.

At one time—could it have been only a week ago?—I would have picked up a pencil and moved it across the paper quickly without hesitation, darkening some areas and highlighting others so that the drawing, whether good or bad, would at least have been alive. This time as I picked up the drawing pencil, nothing happened. That impetus which had always sent my hand dancing over the paper was gone. I drew mechanically, with a line that wandered around the edges of the budding branches, even taking in a bird's nest and a corner of a building across the street, but it was a drawing stillborn.

I tried again. My shoulders stiffened and my head thrust itself forward in concentration. My fingers worked because they were ordered to do so, but the rich, black, fluid lines which had skated effortlessly over the page before refused to come. At last I gave up.

"What's happening, Catherine? Where's that fine dark Italian drawing hand of yours?" Mr. Everett was almost too kind, too attentive.

"I don't know," my voice quivered as he bent over to make a minor correction in the drawing.

"It's not bad, you know. It's just not like you. Don't worry. We all have off days," he said cheerfully.

I smiled weakly and said sure, that was probably it, but I sat there worrying. I tried to believe what he said, that it was only a bad day and that tomorrow I'd be drawing freely again.

Joanna was waiting for me after school. She insisted on taking me to a coffee shop and treating me. We had to talk, she said.

"Some concert our cousin gave, wasn't it?" she began.

"Tony was marvelous."

"He's gonna make it big someday. Okay, so much for small talk. Catherine, what's going on with you?"

"What do you mean?"

"You know what I mean." The green snake eyes demanded an answer.

"Well, I was kicked out of school. I can't take it like you, Jo. Does everyone know?"

"Sure. As if it matters. Half the kids in this school get expelled. It's *that* I'm talking about," she said, pointing to my wrists.

"Does everybody know about that, too?"

"The family does, I think. They guess. They talk. No secrets there. But the kids at school don't know and for heaven's sake, don't tell anyone."

"Don't worry. I won't."

"It was such a dumb thing to do, Cat. *How could you?* Thank God, you flubbed it. If you want to do yourself in that way, you gotta cut real deep. But why did you do it? Why were you expelled? Something to do with the Alcott freak?"

"I can't tell you, but I'm glad you care."

"Care? Cat, I could just about cut my own wrists for not having the brains to know something was wrong and going over to see you. Would it have helped if I had? Tell me the truth."

"Don't blame yourself and don't feel guilty. Yeah, it would've helped, but it's my fault, too. I could have called you, Joanna."

She put her long, slender hand over mine. "Cat, you call me any time you need me, any time you want me, even if it's not important. Will you promise?"

"Thanks. Sure, I promise. And it works the other way, too. Okay?"

So we made a pact. Joanna was my close friend now, I was hers.

"I should have warned you more about that Alcott bitch. She just doesn't make it with people. She's icy cold, Cat, and I can't take that in anyone."

"Anyway, it's all over. I won't see her again. She kicked me out of gym class for good."

"I should be so lucky."

Time was flying and again I'd be late at Mrs. Russo's, but I needed to stay with Joanna. She was helping to bring me back, and I was still needing help, more than I had realized.

"You know, Cat, I been thinking. Someday we'll be out of Gilkie. What do you think, the two of us could live together in New York? Get out of this dump."

The sudden prospect of living somewhere else, of knowing that Gilkie High and Lily Street were not the end, flickered in the indefinite dark of my future.

"I'll think about it," I said lightly, knowing very well I would never live with Joanna. In a curious way we may have loved each other, but she was still the snake and I the tiny bird barely nimble enough to get out of her way. But later, when we left the shop, I carried Joanna's warmth with me. She had given me a gift of herself and I held it closely and thoughtfully.

Saved from the grave, I saw halos everywhere, around Joanna, around my good mother, around my dear aunts and uncles, and even around Mr. Everett and Mrs. Russo. At the end of two weeks, the halos slowly faded and my mother was becoming her familiar self again. Karen Alcott was becoming a disappearing speck and I was getting to the point where I hardly thought of her at all. A burden lifting.

But another burden took her place. I seemed unable to draw anymore. Sitting on the front stoop, I sketched the kids skating down the street on their skateboards, the doorway of the house across the street, and the three weary housecleaning women who chatted on the sidewalk one mellow evening. But the drawings were cold, dead, saying nothing. I begged my mother to sit still for me and she did so in front of the television, moving only to file her fingernails and follow the story on the screen, but that sketch turned out like the others, flat and lifeless.

The child Catherine mocked me from her place on the bedroom wall. Had it been an illusion that I had a gift?

What facility I may have had, first for the dark drawings and then for the light portfolio sketches, was now gone. If I lacked that, then what did I have? What could I look forward to? Possibly I was being punished. If I could not draw, then how could I live? The future was yawning with emptiness.

"Have you gone to confession yet?" my mother nagged. "Catherine, you promised."

"I'll go tomorrow," I promised again.

"As soon as you finish at Mrs. Russo's?"

"Okay, okay, I heard you."

"You must be getting better. You're getting fresh, the way you were before. You know I don't like it when you say, 'Okay, okay, *okay*' like that."

"I can't stand the way you keep after me."

"Someone's got to keep after you, since you don't look after yourself."

We were both more like the way we were, but the sharpness in our voices was not as shrill as before. My mother did not keep on and on, and I did not make faces as I did before.

This time I kept my promise and went to church. I'd almost forgotten how the candles flickered in the dimness and how quiet it was there. First I stopped in front of a statue of the Virgin Mary that stood in an alcove and added my candle to those burning for her. Would it be too greedy to ask forgiveness for my sins, all of them serious, and beg for my "gift" to be returned? It was not to the chipped plaster statue with its traces of gold paint and its insipid expression that I directed my confession, but to the real Mary, the invisible Mary who may have resembled in her kindness my own aunt Mary. I saw her as an early Italian painting, a young earthy woman of strength and compassion.

"Forgive me. I am sorry for everything that happened, for being obsessed, for being foolish, for trying to destroy my life. I promise I'll never do it again."

That statue's eyes were lifted toward the ceiling now as before and her lips did not move. But words came into my head, a message. "What's over is over. You must begin to live your life again as clearly and as well as you can. Be good. Be wise."

The heaven image of Mary faded. Then, though my confession was made, I walked over to the confessional and waited for the priest.

Gradually my wrists healed so that a wide watchband covered the scars on my left wrist and a wide bracelet, given me by my mother, hid the scars on the other wrist.

I was healing in other ways, too. Although my mother did not change radically, nor, I suppose, did I, from time to time she still hugged me unexpectedly and spoke less sharply than before. It still amazed me to think she would have missed me had I gone. Now I listened to her more patiently, though I had a long way to go to become a saint in this regard.

At last I was cured of Karen Alcott. I thought of her less and less each day, until that bittersweet mixture of emotions she had brought into my life came to nothing and I was at last free of the burden of thinking about her. Our paths never crossed.

Therefore it was something of a shock one day in early June, a warm balmy day when everyone was mellowing with the promise of summer, that I nearly bumped into Karen Alcott as I went from one class to another. She was standing in front of Mr. Turner's office and frowning at the class register she held in her hand, as if something did not quite add up, for she bit her lip as she counted and recounted a list of names.

At first my breath stopped now, as it had the first time at the sight of the silky hair loosely tied at the nape of her neck and the grace of her stance. That kind of beauty would haunt me forever. At the same time I saw that a network of wrinkles surrounded her eyes and the two lines that ran from the sides of her nose to the edges of her mouth were deeper and harsher than I remembered. Then too the tautness around her neck, without the softness of the usual scarf that she wore, betrayed her. It was incredible that I had never noticed these details before. So that's one thing that had been wrong with my portraits of her. I was blind. I had not seen her honestly.

"She's old," I was thinking, "so much older than I ever dreamed. And so unhappy."

She was already beginning to resemble all those teachers who had taught too long. With every year she would become dryer, more brittle, less hopeful, and less inclined to smile.

And so my final emotion where Karen Alcott was concerned was that of pity. Incredible that I, of all people, should *pity* Miss Alcott of the expensive silk shirts and white sports car and 29½ Chauncey Circle. She had never become the dancer she imagined herself to be—though I still thought her a beautiful dancer—and now it was too late to think of that career for herself, nor was she a priestess after all nor anything else I had so foolishly imagined, but only a frustrated woman growing older.

At last, completely released, I put a rose over the grave of my adoration and walked past her down the hall. I think she did not even know I had stopped and then moved on.

Chapter Twenty-Five

And then something happened! It was something so good and so entirely unexpected that never again would my mother be able to moan or boast that her life was nothing but a series of tragedies.

One evening in early June she tore into the house, excited tears of joy streaming from her eyes. "It's happened. I won, Cathy. I won!"

"You won the raffle or something? No kidding, which one?"

"Hawaii. Twelve days in Hawaii, sweetie! I coulda died when they picked my number. Everyone was cheering. Hawaii! Wish I could take you with me."

"That's okay, Mom. I'm glad for you. Congratulations!" I hugged her and we danced around. Maybe we weren't losers after all. Maybe sometimes it was possible to win.

My mother, always a dreamer, could never resist buying raffle tickets, entering contests, and investing in lotteries. Until now she had a lifetime record of perfect loss. All her brothers and sisters, even gentle Aunt Mary, annoyed her by telling her how much she had been losing all this time. At last she was justified. Twelve days in Hawaii, all expenses paid—plane fare, expensive hotel on the beach, meals, tickets for tours . . . in short, everything.

The apartment itself lit up with joy. My mother spouted plans. She would go on a diet immediately because the meals there would be so fabulous. She must buy a new wardrobe. What should she bring home to me, perfume or a dress in a bright Hawaiian print? She would be given a *lei* when she arrived, "that string of flowers they put around your neck." Should she buy one and bring it home to me? Maybe she could bring home some plants, some shells. . . .

She stopped short in the middle of her bubbling speculations.

"Catherine, what will you do while I'm away?"

"Nothing. I'll watch over Lily Street and see that it doesn't disappear."

"I can't leave you here alone."

"Mom, you don't have to worry. I'll never do *that* again."

"Who's worried about *that*?" She denied it much too quickly and I knew she would never forget that dreadful night and she would never stop worrying completely. "There are other things, Catherine, all kinds of nuts out there waiting to find a young girl staying home by herself. It would be too lonely for you anyway. Want to stay with Mary? She's crazy about you."

"I know, but she doesn't have the room. I'd be in the way."

"Carol. She's so good-hearted, she'd take you. She's got lots of room and with Gloria in Europe this summer, she'll be glad to have you."

"Mom, I will not go to Aunt Carol's. No way. Could I stay with Nonno and Nonna? They asked me to visit them."

"I never thought of it. You really want to go to the country?"

"Yeah, Mom, I do. It would be a real vacation for me to get out of the city. I'd love it, if they want me. And Mrs.

Russo doesn't need me all that much in the summer. She told me I could have a month off if I liked."

"I'll see," my mother said, quiet now. She seldom went 'home"—where she had spent her childhood—unless it was obligatory, like the family party they had out there every August, and even then she found excuses not to go. Once my mother confided in me about Nonna, who, she said, was too critical. My grandmother favored Carol because she was ambitious and the oldest; she loved Mary, the youngest, because she was so religious and had so many children. My mother, the unfortunate Beatrice, was not only a middle child of no particular talents, but she disgraced her parents by getting a divorce, causing hard feelings that never softened.

Yet I had been named after my grandmother, just as Tony had been named after our grandfather. And so I received the favor that my mother never had. It was there in my grandmother's eyes when we met. I was her Caterina, her *bambina,* her *bella bella,* her *cara carissima.*

My mother telephoned and it was arranged almost immediately that I would stay with Nonna and Nonno. For once everyone was pleased.

School ended and two weeks later my mother would leave for Hawaii. She had also managed to take a few days unearned vacation so that she could stop in California and visit a distant cousin there.

Her enthusiasm was wearing me down. We were pals now, she said, real friends. This meant that I trudged beside her on endless shopping tours. I waited while she tried on thirty shades of lipstick. "Catherine, you're the artist. Tell me which is best, the Romance or the Las Vegas Hot Pink?"

She asked my advice on everything and never followed it. If she held up a dress that screamed with color and I said it was too loud, that satisfied her and she bought it. She bought shoes that would hurt her feet, "*but what heavenly colors,*" she cried. She had to have a seductive black nightgown with insets of lace. I wondered whom she expected to admire her in it, but knew enough to say nothing. Like me, she was a dreamer, a stubborn dreamer.

"It's so good to have a daughter who's a real friend, not just a wild brat like most of the high school kids today," she confided to a salesgirl. Happiness was making her sentimental.

I smiled dutifully and didn't say anything when she said again how remarkable it was we were such great friends now, nor did I have to say a word, for the next minute she was holding up a pair of shrimp-colored sandals and wondering if there'd be room in her luggage for them.

Good luck brings on more good luck! At last my mother was getting her fill of parties. The girls at the office, the bowling team, even my uncle Sal and aunt Julia, all took her out at different times. Aunt Mary invited us for Sunday dinner and the priest came, too. Aunt Carol could not resist the excuse for still another party.

Fortunately this was not one of the more elaborate family affairs, and it rang with a light, festive air. My mother wore a new party dress and planted a gardenia in her hair. She drank too much wine, danced with all her brothers and brothers-in-law, and at one point clowned, shaking her hips in imitation of a hula dancer. For once she was the center of attention and was loving it.

Aunt Carol could not take my mother's joy with entire grace. "Do you know," she announced as though she had not already phoned and told everyone, "that Gloria has won a scholarship and will be going to Europe on an art and fashion tour?"

"So what?" my mother said without thinking, and then pretending it had been a joke, applauded along with everyone else. But I wondered if she were still wishing it was I who had some honor, any honor. At least this time she would not give me the "why-can't-you-be-like-Gloria" treatment. It wasn't honors I was looking for. If only I could draw again, I'd be satisfied.

"Come on, let's dance! Let's have some more wine!" Gloria cried, putting on more records. And so the party went on.

Later as we were getting ready for bed, my mother came into my room with a pack on her face that made it paste-white, and her hair in curlers.

"Catherine, I've been thinking. Maybe something exciting will happen on this trip."

"Exciting like what?"

"I just can't say," she answered, but in her eyes I could see a Hollywood Hawaii with a full moon, palm trees, and a handsome man falling in love with her. My poor mother!

Chapter Twenty-Six

"It's nice, your mamma have vacation," my grandmother was saying as my grandfather drove us home from the airport. We had forty miles yet to go. "Your mamma, she have lots bad luck in her life, some her fault, and some just bad luck. But today, thank God, I see her happy. That plane, ooo, so big!"

"It's-a good luck for her, better luck for us. We get Caterina for nearly three weeks," my grandfather said as he turned around to grin at us in the back seat.

"Hey, you watch-a the road," my grandmother said.

"Tha's-a right. Don't-a worry," my grandfather answered, still grinning at me. I'd never realized before how handsome he really was, with his sun-bronzed skin, a head of thick, curly gray hair and a wide walrus mustache that was fashionable at the moment, although he had worn it that way ever since I could remember, not caring whether or not it was in style.

"I'm so glad you want me to come and stay with you. See, I promised I'd come and here I am," I said.

"Yeah, it's a long time since you come visit us," my grandmother said. "All my grandchildren, so many, so fine, on'y one comes all the time, but I don' tell you who. You have to guess."

"Well, I'm ashamed of myself, staying away so long. But I get busy, Nonna." I excused myself feebly. "There's school and I go to work every day."

"Sure, sure, I unnerstan'. You young, you spring chickie. You should have good time. And now, you got vacation."

As the car turned into the driveway, a dozen white hens shrieked and scattered across the lawn. It pleased me more than I could say that the swing I once played on still hung from a branch of the sugar maple in the front yard. The house rambled and spread, its various parts not quite matching, since the original three-room house had seen many additions and remodelings, because of fires or new babies, which meant there had to be more rooms. A dozen Lily Street apartments like ours could have fit into this farmhouse.

"I love being here again!" I cried, beginning to remember hundreds of things I had long forgotten, the lilac by the back door and the row of peony bushes that bordered the back lawn.

The old lady, my great-grandmother, stood uncertainly at the back door to welcome us as my grandfather parked his ancient Buick. She waved her hand to greet us, whispering her welcome in a hoarse old lady's voice. She was so frail, no bigger than a child, wrinkled, and dressed in black from head to toe. I feared for her delicacy as I bent down to kiss the papery cheek. She leaned on me as we walked slowly, following my grandparents into the kitchen.

"*Novantatre, novantatre,*" she whispered as I helped her settle in a chair.

"Ninety-three, that's how old she is," my grandmother said, as she saw I didn't quite understand. "Your mamma, she didn't teach you Italiano, no?"

I shook my head, ashamed that I couldn't speak it, but I

was still overwhelmed at being at the farm again, taking in the familiarity of the high, whitewashed walls, the square wooden table that stood in the middle of the kitchen; even the cloth that covered it—a heavy cotton tablecloth with red cross-stitching—seemed familiar, as did the houseplants that filled the windows. Even the fragrance of *minestrone verde,* a vegetable soup made with fresh greens, bubbling on top of the old-fashioned gas stove stirred the memory of an earlier time when I was younger than the child in the news-print portrait that hung on my bedroom wall.

My childhood was returning. How could I have forgotten that I lived here once when my mother was ill with a baby that didn't survive after all? Was I four or five or six years old? Had I stayed with my grandparents for one month or six? It was only a cluster of details that I recalled, the treat of a freshly baked *biscotto* or a strawberry dipped in sugar; I must have been deliciously spoiled. Trotting after Nonna, I had helped her make the beds and collect the eggs from the henhouse. Was it that summer or another time that we had picked tomatoes and made great batches of tomato sauce left to cure in the sun while their spices perfumed the yard? A friendly tan dog, Rocco—where was he now? There had been two snow-white goats. I had been allowed to pet a boxful of kittens.

Even now a fat tortoise-shell cat, probably a great-great-great-granddaughter (Have I left out some *great*'s?) of the cat I might have known, rubbed against my legs. I picked her up to pet her and bury my face in her warm fur.

"Nonna, can I sleep in the same room as before?"

"You remember, *cara*? Of course you can stay there. You want to take your bag upstairs, Caterina? Don't stay too long. Tony got to have his lunch and go back to work."

The upstairs bedrooms listed a little this way or that, and

the floors slanted as additions had been made to the house and so strained them, but what must have been most difficult for my grandparents was that those rooms, once filled with children, were now empty. "My room," a corner bedroom from which I could see the small peach orchard, a half-acre vineyard and the pasture where four or five sheep grazed, had not changed at all. The narrow bed with its old-fashioned white seersucker spread, the braided rug on the floor, the small crucifix on the wall, and the red cushion on the rush-bottom chair, remained the same as before. It was only I who was different.

Sitting on the edge of the bed, I figured out that I must have been four or five when I stayed here before, days of innocence before the first grade when I learned that I had a "gift." A puzzle. I had always believed it, been sure of it. I knew that many of the drawings in the portfolio were good. And yet Karen Alcott had told me I had no talent. And then I could not draw anymore, only strained lifeless things. And what was the truth?

"Hey, Caterina, we goin' to have lunch now," my grandmother called up the stairs.

I brushed my hair and put on a smile for everyone. The four of us sat around the kitchen table and my grandmother pinched my cheek affectionately. My grandfather ate his soup noisily, "zouping it in," as my mother called it, and the great-grandmother crumpled bread in her soup. She had no teeth, but it didn't stop her from enjoying her lunch.

"Don't let your grandmother work you too hard," my grandfather warned, half-joking in order to get a rise out of my grandmother.

"It's all right with me, Nonno," I said. "Here work is like playing."

"Like *playing*. What you talk about, Caterina?"

My grandmother paid no attention to my grandfather's ribbing. She removed the soup plates from the table when we were finished and brought on a glass bowl filled with perfect red strawberries.

"Fragole al limone!" she announced proudly. "From my garden!"

My grandfather grunted approval and stopped talking while he relished each berry, ended his lunch with a last swallow of table wine, and got up reluctantly to go back to work.

"Still at the same place? What are you doing these days, Nonno?"

"The same like always. Driving the tractor."

For over fifty years now he managed the crops and ran the operations on the fields of a large model farm. It was his first job when he came over from a small village in southern Italy when he was eighteen years old, and this was the job he had held all his working life. My grandmother, not much older than I was, had worked as cleaning maid in the big farmhouse.

It had never occurred to me before to realize what courage it must have taken to travel to a strange distant country without any money and without knowing the language. My grandfather still signed his name with an X and at home they talked only in Italian. Here they stayed in the same place, buying land whenever they could and raising a family of ten children while the seasons came and went. Of the ten children, only nine remained, and all of them produced grandchildren, but not one lived on the farm or near it.

"Don' work too hard, Caterina. Remember, it's vacation!" my grandfather said as he placed a weathered straw hat on his head and left.

Great-grandmother crumpled an anise cake in her coffee and sipped the hot liquid with frequent "ah's" while I helped Nonna with the dishes.

"Tell me now 'bout Mamma and your brother, Vincie. I never see him. Not turn out so good, huh?"

She confided that she had never wanted my mother to marry my father. "A nice man in his way, good-looking, but I tell yo' mother, it wouldn' work. You think she listen? My other daughters, yes. Not Beatrice. She want to get married, leave the farm like the others, live in the city," my grandmother said sadly. There must have been some frightful arguments then.

"Well, Nonna..." I began to say and checked myself. I tended to be on my mother's side, for all that I adored Nonna. I wanted to get away from home, too. Did daughters always fight with mothers? My mother thought typing would be my salvation, but I knew I would never study it to please her and fill out her ambitions. I wondered, did my grandmother listen to *her* mother when she kissed her good-bye and left to go to America never to return? Someday I would ask her that, but not now, not yet.

"Sons, they do what they like. Is all right," she went on, "but with girls, it's not the same. They should obey."

"But can't mothers make mistakes? Are daughters always wrong?" I asked, keeping my voice mild so she wouldn't think I wanted to argue.

When the dishes were finished, my grandmother helped the old lady to her bed in the sunroom. "Caterina, *tesoro,* I'm busy, okay? You go outside, walk around, lie in the hammock, do what you like. Okay?" She kissed me on both cheeks the way she did when I was a tiny child. It was good to be "home" once more!

I took off my shoes and socks and walked barefoot through the grassy backyard, eventually settling in the hammock suspended between two apple trees. After years of Lily Street, I could hardly believe air could be so fragrant.

Had my drawings been as good as I'd thought at the time,

I wondered, or had it all been an illusion? Would I draw again? I was not sorry I'd burned the Alcott drawings; better to have destroyed them, the good ones along with the bad. My past was burned and the future had not begun.

The tortoise-shell cat jumped up neatly, landing beside me and purring. "Wise cat, never worried, never upset. Is it enough to purr and sleep and catch a bird or a mouse once in a while?" Well then, the cat would become my teacher. For three weeks I'd forget about drawing and do nothing more than sleep, purr, and be petted. And so I took a nap in the warm afternoon.

Nonna did not mean to wake me, she said, as she passed by an hour later. A white kerchief was tied around her head and fastened in back. "Caterina, don' get up. Your mamma tol' me you didn' sleep las' night. A late party and then you get up early to get to the airport. I'm jus' goin' to pick the last peas. They'll be a leetle old, a leetle tough maybe, but good enough."

"Let me go with you."

I picked up a battered saucepan that lay on the ground at the end of the row. Together we stood on either side of the vines that climbed on wires and picked what remained of the peas. From time to time my hand brushed my grandmother's hand reaching for the same pod, and once she seized my hand, which was squat and strong, like hers. Her dark eyes peeped through the vines.

"*Carissima!* You fine girl. Pretty girl!"

"Me? But I'm not pretty, Nonna."

"What's that you say? You a beautiful girl."

"You don't think I look like a monkey?"

"How you talk! You look-a like me and I'm no monkey. If you think you're monkey, then tha's what you are. But you, Caterina d'Amato. No monkey. You be proud."

Me, proud? What a joke!

"When I go in the house," my grandmother continued, "I find picture from Italy to show you. Then you see, you and me, the same."

Since she had always seemed very old, it never occurred to me that I could possibly resemble her, but of course it was from her that my upturned nose, my too-large eyes, and small stubborn chin had come. Her lips curled easily at the corners into a smile; did mine do that, too? From time to time a certain sadness appeared in her eyes. Had I inherited that as well?

As I reached for the last pod on the vine, time telescoped itself. I was myself, Catherine d'Amato, but also an extension of my grandmother, who had been an extension of her mother and so on back, back, and still further back. It might have been centuries ago that a wide-footed, strong Italian girl was picking peas in the hot afternoon sun on a farm somewhere in southern Italy, and in a way I was that very girl here on a farm in Connecticut. This revelation led to still other insights, such as that I did not exist alone but through the grace of others. If this line of strong-footed Italian girls had stopped with me, would that have been morally wrong? I wondered. Then my grandmother interrupted my train of thought.

"Caterina, what's that on your wrist, those lines? And the other wrist, too?"

I pulled my hands down immediately to hide the scars, but it was too late. She saw them. She knew. My sin would follow me forever.

"It's nothing. An accident. It happened a long time ago."

"Caterina! Is no accident," she whispered in a shocked voice.

"I went to confession, Nonna. I promised I'd never do it again. I promised God."

If she asked me why, I wouldn't know how to answer, but

she was so upset she could say nothing at all. Silently we took
our pans of peas and walked slowly to the worn table in the
backyard and there we sat on benches, shelling peas into a
blue-speckled enamel bowl. It had been very careless of me
to let her see the scars, but it couldn't be helped now. Neither
of us spoke. After a while she stood up.

"I almos' forgot. I want to show you picture of me when
I got married at home in Italy, jus' before I come here to
this country."

She disappeared and in a few moments came from the
house with a folder. Inside, a formal sepia portrait showed a
solemn young Caterina in the clothes of another time. She
stood beside a small round table and held a bouquet of flowers in her hand. An impetuous mass of curly black hair was
tied and pinned to the back of her head and the eyes that
blazed out of the picture burned with defiance and courage.

"It's me. See, just like-a you."

A tremor passed through me. Here was proof. It could
have been my portrait, but did I have such courage?

"Tell me, Nonna. When you got married, when you and
Nonno decided to leave Italy, were you scared?"

"*Mamma mia,* was I scared! My mother and father were
begging me. Don' go, they said, we don' see you again. Relatives were telling me the boat would sink or that I'd starve
when I got here, that there were wild Indians. Such nonsense!" She shook her head and grinned. "I almos' gave in,
I was that afraid. But Tony and I, we decided we'd go. And
I thought would be better here, and is so. You make up your
mind, you go. That's all! You like-a this picture? I give it
to you."

"But it's so precious, Nonna. It's you as a young girl. As
a bride."

"If you like, I want you to keep it."

"Oh, Nonna, thank you! I love it. I'd rather have this than anything in the world."

I would keep it forever to remind me that in these Caterinas, there was more courage than fear. It had worked for Caterina Martini. And for me? I had yet to find that out.

Chapter Twenty-Seven

Three days passed. I was becoming a country girl, getting nicely tanned.

"We make strawberry jam today before the strawberries are over. This year the berries are bee-yoo-ti-ful!" My grandmother kissed her fingers in admiration of her crop.

Her halting English more often than not gave way to Italian, which she kept telling me I must learn. Some of it I understood, particularly when she made exaggerated gestures to explain it. For the most part I didn't catch it, but I was loving the music of it. I wanted to learn Italian, and when I spoke a few phrases to her or to my grandfather, they were pleased.

"Let me help. I can pick berries."

"You don't have to. This is your vacation, *cara.* But you should know how to make jam. Someday when you get married and have children, you'll want to know such things."

I laughed because it would be one long time before I had a husband and children to make jam for. Early in the morning we walked out to the strawberry beds and admired the drops of dew on the leaves and grass as they twinkled in the sun. My grandmother picked the plump berries *presto,* one, two, three, and I did too at first, but then dawdled and dreamed. Once I dug both hands into the crumbly dark soil and watched an earthworm escape into the ground to safer quarters.

Why should the soil feel so good on my hands? Because it was "real"? If "real" meant the opposite of the Mona Lisa with its false marble decor and the air full of chemicals disguised with cloying sweetness, then this earth was real. The red-heart berries nestled against an exuberance of green leaves, and my grandmother was picking them off at a tremendous rate. I watched her hands pick a berry or two, drop them in the basket, and go after the next.

"Wait, Nonna, hold it."

"Hold what?"

"Your hands, the way they are. If you'll let me, I'd like to draw them. I'll go get my sketchbook."

"My hands. You want to draw my hands?" she asked, amazed, holding them out as if she had never seen them before. "Ah, you like my manicure, maybe? The dirt under the nails?"

At least this amused her. I ran to my room and flew back out into the garden again with sketchbook and pencil. By this time she had picked another basket of fruit. I rearranged her hands and she held them patiently while I drew them among the leaves, the fingers of one holding the berry as she plucked it from the stem. The sketch was imperfectly drawn, but it flowed.

"Please, just one more, Nonna," I begged. This time I moved back far enough to see my grandmother kneeling in the morning sun among the berry leaves. The sketch could have been good or bad, but it felt sound. It moved. Not daring to do anymore, as if afraid to exercise too vigorously after a long illness, I left the sketchbook and spent the rest of the day picking berries and making jam.

"When you make jam, Nonna, you sure do it in a big way. So many jars!" I told my grandmother.

"And you are like me. I think maybe when you draw pictures, you make a hundred. How do you think I know this? I tell you little secret. Anthony, he tol' me you are very good. Like my grandfather and my uncle Vincenzo. They were artists, very good artists. What, you didn' know that?"

I made a number of sketches during the day but it wasn't until late afternoon that I dared to examine them. They were hardly dramatic, like the black drawings I used to do, nor flighty like some of the portfolio drawings, but they were solid and alive, unlike anything I'd ever drawn before. I could feel the strength and tenderness in my grandmother's hands and the sun shining on them, making highlights and shadows. I was drawing what I saw, what I knew, and what I felt, and it was the truth. I was the Catherine d'Amato here and I was all the other Caterinas, too. My life would be different from theirs, as theirs had probably been different from their mothers and grandmothers, but that's where it began, knowing where I came from.

Lesson One. I was beginning to know who I was, and this new awareness pleased me. I sighed with relief that at last I had discovered what had been there all the time.

Lesson Two. It was my grandmother who was helping me, but it was my drawings that made me know. It was not a matter of "the gift" or "the talent." I did not have to worry about whether it was there or not. If my drawing spoke the truth, that's all that mattered.

For nearly three weeks I became a country Catherine, feeding the chickens, collecting the eggs, making jams and relishes with Nonna, picking vegetables from the garden and helping my grandmother put them away in her large freezer in the garage. By now I could speak a little Italian. With Nonno, Nonna, and the little great-grandmother forever telling me something and repeating it until I understood, I had no choice but to learn it.

That little great-grandmother made me understand she wanted me to sneak forbidden anise cakes and little candies to her!

I also sketched, filling the sketchbooks I had brought along with me.

"Caterina, are you homesick, maybe a little?" my grandmother asked. "You don't miss your mamma?"

"Sure I miss her," I said faithfully, although I could have used another three weeks of vacation. "On the post cards, she says she's having a good time." Distance softens discords and I would not be sorry to see her again. I wondered if she was finding that romance she was seeking, but I wasn't in a hurry to get back to Lily Street.

The next day my grandmother was up earlier than usual, and when I came downstairs, she smiled mischievously.

"What's that for? Something's going on, isn't it?"

"I don't know," she said, though of course, she did. "You'll see."

My grandfather's eyes twinkled and the tiny great-grandmother mumbled in Italian and grinned, but nobody let me in on the secret. That morning they were cooking, cooking, cooking—making ravioli and stuffing a roast of lamb with garlic and the sweet leaves of *basilico* which grew outside the kitchen door.

"I know the secret. You've invited the U.S. Army to dinner."

"Maybe. Could be," my grandmother said.

At noon I decided to walk to the village to get a new sketchbook at the drugstore, since the ones I had brought

with me were now filled with landscapes, line drawings of
the animals, ink studies of my grandparents and of my great-
grandmother, who chuckled with pleasure as I drew her.

"It's a long walk. More than two mile'," my grandmother
said.

"I don't mind," I said, becoming sorry somewhat later as
the hot road stretched on before me and I perspired under the
red kerchief wound around my head. When I reached the
store, I revived with a cold root beer, bought a sketchbook
and two bags of licorice and gumdrops to help satisfy my
great-grandmother's sweet tooth. Then I faced the hot road
back.

The sun gleamed on the pavement. A grass snake wriggled
across the road and disappeared. I was enjoying the hot afternoon silence, broken mostly by the sounds of insects and bird
calls and the mooing of cows in the distance, when the intense drone of a motorcycle sent me flying to the side of the
road. The motorbike stopped up ahead, then turned around
and headed toward me slowly. The helmeted figure yelled at
me, stopped, and jumped off the bike.

"Tony, is that you? On this thing?"

"Sure, why not? And what are you doing here?" I could
tell by the way he was smiling, he must have known all along
that I was here.

"So you're the big surprise Nonna was telling me about."

"She was being cagy about the surprise she had for *me*."

"And you're so smart. You guessed without thinking twice,
didn't you?"

"No secrets in the family. How's it going?"

"Terrific, Tony. I love it here so far. Where'd you get the
BMW? It's a beauty."

"Borrowed it. But don't tell my parents or my violin
teacher. He's terrified something will happen to me. This
would give him a heart attack."

"No wonder. You're precious property. I've never been on one of those things."

"Time to start then. Climb on."

I snuggled against his strong back as we flew down one country road and up another. Of course this was the grandchild who visited frequently, for he knew the area well. He took me to a small lake, to an abandoned stone house and then to a strange village half-hidden amid fields and groves of trees and pastures. He rode fast. It was as close to flying as I'd ever come. I wanted to stay on this fast metal stallion forever and ever, but it was to Nonna's we were going, so after a long while, we swung around and headed back toward the farm.

It was a unique feeling, this pure happiness.

Anthony's visit was brief, for he had to return to the city that night. The following day he would be moving to New York. That night we sat around the table, decorated with its best embroidered cloth, to share a last dinner. My great-grandmother, feeling weak, decided to stay in bed, so there were only four of us.

"Two Caterinas, two Antonios. It is perfect," my grandmother said.

My grandfather gave the blessing and we raised our glasses to drink his homemade *vino*, wishing the best to one another and to the future. Silently I gave thanks to be in this place which was truly my home and for the three people I loved so much and for their love for me. Upstairs in my room were sketchbooks filled with good drawings. Never before had I felt so rich.

"Caterina, Tony, one word before we eat. This is your home. Never forget it, eh? Caterina and Tony, you come here as much as you like. You are the special ones," my grandmother said.

"Listen to your grandmother. For once she speaks good sense," my grandfather said.

Nonna grinned broadly, then insisted on heaping our plates with food.

"Too much, Nonna! You're spoiling us. You'll make me fat!" Tony cried.

But it was not of food but of Tony's career that we spoke. His eyes glowed as he told us about the music school he would be attending in New York and about the enormous scholarship that had been granted to him. Ten thousand dollars.

"Ten t'ousand dollar! A miracle!" my grandfather cried.

While I helped with the dishes afterward, my grandfather insisted that Tony play *his* violin from Italy, the one he insisted was a Cremona, although Tony winked to let me know this was an old man's fantasy. Nevertheless he took the violin and shocked everyone by bursting into an out-of-tune scraping such as any beginner might make, appearing to be so serious about it that even I was taken aback, wondering what had happened to him, until, grinning broadly, he burst into a series of leaping arpeggios so brilliant that the hair rose on the back of my neck. My grandfather said, "See, see! It's my good violin that makes such good music."

Then Tony strolled into the kitchen, playing some old country dances to please Nonna, who put down her dishtowel and danced a few steps to show him she could still get around.

"That music, thassa old stuff," she said, though it was easy to see she loved it. "Play something new, Tony! Play the song I love most, you know what I like."

The evening flew. Nonna insisted that I show Tony my sketches. At first I was reluctant, fearing that Tony might find fault with them, giving them the thumbs-down no matter how kindly he would do it. But he begged to see what I was doing, so I brought down the sketchbooks.

Tony turned over the pages, smiled at a funny drawing of the chickens running, gravely examined a pen-and-ink sketch of the great-grandmother, and nodded at the others, even those through which I'd put a large X to show I thought they hadn't quite come across. However, most of them worked.

"I knew you could do it," Tony said. "You're okay now. I always liked your work. Those dancers were good. But when you drew that teacher, you went way off. I never knew what got into you. Anyway, these drawings are genuine. They sing. Really good, Cat. Thanks for letting me see them."

"You two, you the best of all," Nonna said. "So good you are here. But Tony leaves and then Caterina..."

Her eyes filled with tears, something rare for Nonna, and for Nonno too as they said good-bye to Tony and blessed him.

Tony and I walked outside. The night air was soft and caressing.

"So it's New York for you! It will be wonderful. You think about it for years and it seems far away, and then suddenly it's right there," I said.

"I know. I can hardly believe it. And you, Cat, what will happen to you?"

"Well, first I finish high school. And then..." but I wasn't hesitating. Somewhere in the last week I woke up knowing exactly what I would do, but I hadn't dared to tell anyone until now.

"And then I'm going to get a scholarship to a good art school if I can. I hope it will be in New York, but I'll take what I can get. What do you think?"

"It's what I expected all along. You worried me when you got off the track, but... what made you become so certain all of a sudden?"

"I can't say," I said, but of course I could. It was what I had seen in the sepia photograph of Nonna, that courage stronger than fear. She went to a strange land because she felt she must. I would do the same thing.

"If you came to New York during the year, Cat, you could see what it's like. My aunt would put you up for a weekend. Then you could go to museums; you *should* see them, really. Maybe visit art schools. I'd introduce you to people. Will you come?"

"If it's all right with you and your aunt, sure!"

We were walking along the edge of the pasture by a rail fence. A horse walked over to stare at us. We plucked some sweet grass and held it out to him.

"You know, Cat, you and I will always have something between us that's different. We're of the family, but we're set apart, too."

"In the way that Nonna and Nonno were set apart from their families. Maybe that's what they see in us. Do you ever get scared?"

"A little shaky when I think of it. But not really. If you're going to be an artist, Cat, you don't have much choice. That's it."

"I understand. Tony, even if we go far away, let's always remember to come back to Nonna and Nonno. And all the others, too. At least, I would want to."

"Of course."

Our slow walk ended at his motorcycle. "Cat, we'll keep in touch. Remember, you'll come to New York some weekend?"

"Sure. Thanks, Tony. Good luck!" He kissed me in a brief, brotherly way, adjusted his helmet and roared off down the country road.

I walked slowly back to the house. The pasture was spread out in front of me, wide and clear, silvery in the moonlight. I paused at the fence. The horse had moved far over the hill, so I was alone. An unexpected thought came to me: "I am Catherine d'Amato and that's all right. It's good."

On the morning of the last day, my grandmother sat on the bench in the grape arbor so I could sketch her. It was a hot day and I think she did not feel too well, but she insisted on sitting for me for this last sketch. I could not tell then that she would not live through the coming winter. I thought of her as existing forever and forever.

"I'll come to see you again, soon," I promised late that afternoon as I put my suitcase in the back of my grandfather's car. The three of us kissed my tiny great-grandmother goodbye and then drove away. A certain sadness mingled with sweetness, so that we could hardly talk until we arrived at the airport to meet my mother's plane.

Winifred Madison has written thirteen books for children and young people and has taught courses in writing through the University of California. Something she particularly enjoys is leading a workshop for young writers.

A Portrait of Myself is not autobiographical and has nothing to do with the author's own background or experiences. Mrs. Madison is an artist, but she did not begin to draw until after she finished college. Since then she has exhibited paintings and batiks, which have been widely shown in northern California and elsewhere. She was brought up in Connecticut but has spent much of her life in Davis, California.